MURDER
MACHREE

Also by Eleanor Boylan
in Thorndike Large Print

Working Murder
Murder Observed

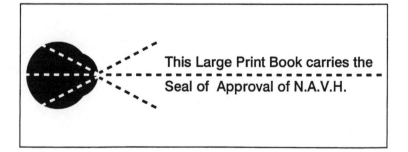

MURDER MACHREE

ELEANOR BOYLAN

Thorndike Press • Thorndike, Maine

Library of Congress Cataloging in Publication Data:

Boylan, Eleanor.
    Murder Machree / Eleanor Boylan.
        p. cm.
    ISBN 1-56054-447-3 (alk. paper : lg. print)
    1. Large type books. I. Title.
[PS3552.O912M79   1992b]   92-11070
813'.54—dc20   CIP

Thorndike Press Large Print edition published in 1992
by arrangement with Henry Holt and Company, Inc.

Cover design by Marjorie Cormier.

The tree indicium is a trademark of Thorndike Press.

This book is printed on acid-free, high opacity paper. ∞

MURDER MACHREE

1

"It's quite a story, Armand," said my son, Henry, breaking the shocked silence.

Henry's wife, Tina, said, "Yes, it has lots of goodies like mystery and scandal and sex — practically everything except," she added lightly, "murder."

Armand Evers sipped his drink. He said, "That may be coming."

Another silence, this one even more uncomfortable. Was he putting us on? My daughter, Paula, said, with a little laugh, "Oh, neat. It really wouldn't be complete without a murder. Whose?"

"Mine," said Armand.

I choked gently but purposely on my cognac, and everybody laughed, which relieved the strain.

The hot summer night should long since have driven us from the screened porch to the inside cool of the cottage, but Armand's account, complete with brandishing cigar and

7

vibrations of his venerable voice, had held the six of us trancelike, as the listeners are held at the beginning of *The Turn of the Screw.*

Armand, giving no indication that he thought we were treating his story frivolously, pointed to a briefcase I hadn't noticed lying on the floor beside him. "It's all in there," he said. "What I want Clara to do is to read it — I may have left out some in the telling — and decide whose daughter Rachael really is."

"Rachael?" I said. The name, that of Armand's sister, a dear friend of mine, hadn't come into the account.

"Yes." Armand moved on his canvas chair. "I substituted the name Rose because I didn't want to shock you right off the bat. Yes, Rachael. My sister."

Nobody laughed this time, and my cousin, Charles Saddlier, known affectionately all his long life as "Sadd," came erect on the chaise longue, his thick white hair catching the gleam of the one low porch light. He said, dating himself, " 'Tain't funny, McGee."

No, Armand agreed, it wasn't. The red eye of his cigar trembled a little in the dark. "And it may sound even less funny before we're through. But if Rachael's mother and mine aren't the same person, it's important to know."

8

This time the silence was downright desperate. Then my son-in-law, Andy, hoisted his chubby form from the floor beside Paula's chair and said, "Refills, anybody? . . . Then let's swim."

The mundanely cheerful suggestion was just what was needed. Andy and Henry collected glasses and took orders, and Tina and Paula went inside to check on their children. Armand and Sadd and I sat in the warm darkness. I said, "Armand, I really want no part —"

"I adore Cape Cod." Armand stretched his long legs. "You and Henry always used to take a cottage here in August, didn't you?"

"Yes, this one. Armand —"

"But Sadd and Harriet were Bar Harbor people like us. Sadd, do you remember —"

"Armand . . ." Sadd's voice was dry. "Clara is making a justifiable attempt to get at why —"

"My mother's family had always preferred the Adirondacks." No hint in his voice of embarrassment or hurry. "Lake George was not only fashionable but beautiful — one can't say that for all resorts — and Mother loved to paint. Clara, you still paint, I hope?"

"Dammit, Armand —"

But I was thwarted by Andy, who came out carrying a tray of drinks. Armand began extolling the excellence of the beer, and I gave

9

up. Sadd shrugged and lay back on the chaise, and I asked Andy to tell Armand about his job with a film company. Armand, I vaguely recalled, had been involved with theater.

It had begun as a particularly pleasant day, a "fun" day, we all agreed, although Sadd, retired publisher and watchdog of everybody's syntax, wouldn't have it; "fun" was a noun, not an adjective. A day could be "full of fun" or "fun-filled," but not — by which time the kids were halfway up the beach. In any event, the whole week had been a delightful, sunny, salty one in Chatham, where I'd taken my usual cottage for the month of August. Sadd, up from his home in Florida, was sharing it with me, and I'd invited my children and grandchildren for the final week.

Armand had invited himself. Himself and his murder.

I looked at the dim outline of his profile and wondered if I'd have recognized Armand Evers had he appeared at my door unannounced. Possibly not, though his rangy form was reminiscent of his sister Rachael's. It was years since I'd seen any of the Evers family. Rachael and I had been close friends in our youth, but she had spent all of her married life in Ireland, and distance had whittled our contact to occasional though cordial correspondence.

What had possessed Armand to air the scandalous goings-on in his family's history? And if Rachael's parentage was in question, I'd prefer to be the last to know.

Yesterday I'd received a letter from him forwarded from my brownstone in New York City. He'd found my name in the phone book but had failed to reach me. He hoped I remembered him. He was in from his home in Rochester and staying at the Dorrence on the Upper West Side. Could he see me about a rather delicate family matter? He remembered that Henry Gamadge had sometimes advised on such things, but he'd heard Henry had died and perhaps I could help. Would I call him?

I had done so that morning in a dripping bathing suit, said I was vacationing with my family at the Chatham Bars cottages but would be back in New York in a few days and would be glad to call him.

At four o'clock he had phoned from the Hyannis airport.

What *was* this? Sadd, who had known the Evers boys better than I, said he remembered Armand as "impulsive." To say the least. I was very irritated, despite the fact that he firmly declined to be fetched at the airport and had arrived at our cottage in a taxi ladened with wine, candy, and some rather expensive beach toys.

My grandchildren had been torn from the latter, fed, and put to bed when Armand, with whom I'd told the family I'd be closeted on a "delicate family matter," looked around with an expansive gesture and said, "Gather round, my friends, and anyone who wants the rights to this tale may have them. I'll take a mere ten percent of the TV miniseries."

There was stunned silence. Family matter? Delicate? My son, daughter, and their spouses looked at me askance but sat down. Sadd, frowning heavily, stretched on the chaise. I sat beside Armand and kept my eyes on the moonlit stretch of beach between the porch and the ocean. I was mortified by this exhibition, and although I could hardly send Armand packing without more embarrassment to us all, I decided to do so directly when he was finished.

The gist of his story was this:

In the spring of the year 1885, the Boyd Evers family of New York City and Saratoga Springs was plunged into a wretched situation that, if not exactly anticipated, had long been a dreaded possibility. Their only consolation was the fact that their dear friends and neighbors on Tenth Street, Mr. and Mrs. Theodore Roosevelt, parents of the rising young Theodore Jr., were enduring a similar martyrdom: their son Elliott had added to his many escapades the seduction of one of their own parlor maids, and the girl was making understandable claims regarding her expected child. Elliott's father and his brother, Theodore Jr., were attempting to deal with the situation honorably though quietly, particularly for the sake of Elliott's little daughter, Eleanor.

Simultaneously, Boyd Evers, Jr., had presented his family with a like problem, the difference being that the girl in question was no parlor maid but a promising young actress in the New York production of *The Importance of Being Earnest.* She had a fairly high profile and equally high expectations should she be required to go abroad for "reasons of health" or "to study her art" or for whatever purpose most compatible with a large endowment from the Evers family. Like Elliott, Boyd had an honorable father and a brother, named Armand, who undertook to subsidize the required absence, and the girl went off to Paris. A year later she returned with the sad news for the Evers family that the baby had died at birth, but with the glad news for the press that she had met a titled Frenchman during her year of study and was returning to France to marry him.

This she apparently did, and was not heard from again. But Mrs. Evers and Mrs. Roosevelt, despondently comparing notes, won-

13

dered which was worse: the parlor maid's living child, a constant source of mortification, or the actress's dead one, which, ghastly possibility, might not be dead at all but ticking away somewhere in the world, ready to be produced if the need arose.

Meanwhile, Boyd and his brother, Armand, had, in 1890, married the wealthy Marbury sisters of Grosse Pointe. They had one son each, and it was in this generation that the genes had done one of those unaccountable turnabouts. Riotous, rakish Boyd fathered that model of rectitude Boyd Evers III, who, after a distinguished career in the ministry, and an idyllic marriage that produced Boyd IV, died a much loved bishop. That model of rectitude Armand produced riotous, rakish Armand Jr., who from boyhood "scrapes" went on to lacerate perpetually the feelings of his family by borderline involvements with the law until, in 1916, he stabbed a croupier in Monte Carlo in a quarrel over a casino waitress. His distraught father and his pregnant wife, Julia, went to France to help extricate Armand Jr. from these difficulties, those involving the waitress proving rather more complicated than expected, as she too was pregnant. They found that Armand had enlisted. To the great relief of the entire family he was killed at Château-Thierry two months later. The year was 1918.

His wife returned to Grosse Pointe and to her three-year-old son, Armand (sitting before us), bringing her infant daughter, Rachael, with her. But was Rachael the child of Julia Evers or of the nameless waitress of Monte Carlo? Presumably only Julia knew. Her pregnancy had been touch and go. . . . And had the French girl wanted a child? The small town in France where these events took place was heavily shelled, and records were lost — at which point in the account Sadd said *that* plot went out with Wilkie Collins.

But I was not in the mood to joke. Why, after seventy-odd years, need the question be brought up at all? I glanced with distaste at the briefcase. Records, after all? Possible proof? And why this obnoxiously public performance? Was Armand for some reason resentful of the sister he'd always seemed fond of? Was he spiteful? Even a bit deranged?

He certainly seemed neither as he laughed now and said to Andy, "Okay, if you're a thirties movie buff, answer me this — and I can check you because it's my all-time favorite: What movie, starring Charles Boyer and Jean Arthur, climaxed in the sinking of a transatlantic liner —"

"And featured Colin Clive and Leo Carrillo. *History Is Made at Night.*" Andy looked smug and Armand slapped his knee.

Sadd said, "I was in love with Jean Arthur for years."

"Me too," said Armand. "That voice."

As the conversation turned to movies, Henry and Tina came back in swimsuits. I had a fleeting hope that Armand had been playing a trick on us. His theater background — it was coming back to me now — had involved writing and producing. Was this a rather tasteless ploy to get ideas? Would he at any moment say, "Forgive me, the truth is you've just heard my first two acts and I'm stuck for a third"?

But he only said, as Paula came out carrying her three-month-old daughter, "And what is this angel's name?"

"This is Andrea," said Paula. "Mom, will you give her this bottle while we swim?"

The moonlight swim was a nightly ritual. It gave me enormous pleasure to watch the four of them race down the beach and plunge into the black and foamy water. You know that your children must face, have faced, will face, their own pain; and to be able to provide, even occasionally, a sliver of happiness, a splinter of fun, and watch it being enjoyed . . .

And now Armand had dumped on it.

He was standing up looking through the screen where the bugs beat. Shouts came from

16

the water. I adjusted the baby to the crook of my arm and said, "Armand, I'll call the inn and see if they have a room. I'd put you up, but there isn't a square inch. And please take this back with you." I indicated the briefcase. "I really want no part —"

"By golly, that looks like fun!" Armand chuckled, gazing across the beach. "I wish I'd brought my suit — I'd join 'em."

Thank heaven you didn't, I thought. That would only prolong the visit. To my dismay, Sadd said, "Borrow mine."

Was he mad?

Armand turned eagerly. "Sadd, you're a prince! Where is it?"

I shook my head violently at Sadd; I'd have preferred my fist, but one clutched the baby and the other the bottle.

"It's on a nail next to the outdoor shower in the back. The light switch is inside the kitchen door. It will take me longer to get out of this chaise than it will take you to find it."

"Don't budge." Armand laughed and departed. Sadd called after him, "Change in my room — right off the kitchen. You'll have more privacy than I've had all week."

I was fuming. "I can't believe you've done this! Why would you want that man here one more minute?"

17

"I don't, of course. But this gives you a chance to phone Rachael."

Jolted, I allowed the bottle to wander from the baby's mouth. She protested and I drove it back. I said, "Rachael happens to live in Dublin, Ireland."

"Where I believe they have telephones."

It was such a surprising though sensible suggestion that I had to gather my wits for a few seconds. Then I said, "What shall I say to her?"

"Well, you don't begin with 'How are you, Rachael, and are you your father's illegitimate daughter?' "

"Don't joke — it's too awful. His own sister." I lifted Andrea to my shoulder and patted away, probably rather too vehemently. "And that account of his father's shenanigans — not to mention 'everyone's relief' when the man was killed in the war. How can I broach the thing to Rachael?"

"How long since you've seen her?"

I thought back. "She came to New York once after her husband died, so . . . ten years. But we write regularly."

Sadd said, "You want to find out if she knows Armand is doing this. When did she last see him? Are they on good terms? You tell her that he dropped in and you got to talking about old times and it was so pleasant

18

you thought you'd give her a call, and so forth."

I said, applying the bottle to Andrea again, "Bring me the portable phone. I think it's in Tina and Henry's room. He was using it this morning."

"Hadn't we better wait till we know he's headed for the beach?" Sadd struggled out of the chaise, swearing colorfully — but of course grammatically — about stiff joints. "Remind me not to sit in one of those things again."

"I know. I avoid them, too. It takes a derrick." I stared at my granddaughter's beautiful brow. "Sadd, how do you explain all this?"

"I don't. I can't."

I peered past the dark recesses of the living room to the lighted little back hall. Armand walked across it carrying the swimsuit and pulling off his shirt. I said, "It's his crudeness. When he wrote to me he indicated a need for privacy and tact, and now we've had this squalid exposé. It's almost as if" — Armand, changing, cast a gesticulating shadow on the floor of the hall — "as if he suddenly wanted witnesses."

"Testifiers. The word *witness* implies —"

"All I know is he went from private to public when he knew we were all here."

The baby's eyes were slits of contentment. Appetite appeased, drowsiness rushing in, a state devoutly to be wished. I put the bottle on the floor and stood up.

"Give her to me," Sadd said.

I concealed my surprise — Sadd was a baby avoider par excellence — and laid Andrea in his arms, never taking my eyes from the hall where Armand's shadow still performed.

"That business about his own upcoming murder is pure theatrics," Sadd said. "Who'd want to murder him — except possibly you. I mean, what for?"

I allowed my eyes to go to the briefcase, then back to the hall again. Armand appeared, thin and white-chested, and vanished out the back door. Seconds later he rounded the cottage, waving a towel.

"I stole this," he called, and trotted down the beach.

Sadd said, "Make the call to Ireland before he dives in that water and has to be lugged back here with cardiac arrest."

I took the sleeping Andrea from him and went into the little front bedroom where the rented crib stood beside her parents' bed. Moving carefully in the dark, I stepped over her five-year-old sister Janey's bedroll and laid the baby down. The window afforded me a faint glimpse of Armand standing uncertainly on the water's edge. There was no sign or sound of the young people. Had they gone on up the beach? Oh, Lord, don't let him plunge friskily in alone and end up murdered indeed by his own foolishness.

I turned from the crib and now noticed, my eyes more accustomed to the dark, that the bedroll was empty. Sleeping arrangements had not been the same two nights in a row, and I'd managed, only by threat of eviction, to maintain my own bed. I walked through the connecting bathroom, stumbling over a sneaker and a plastic sailboat, and into Henry and Tina's room. I snapped on the ceiling light. Ten-year-old Hen had eschewed his bedroll and appropriated his parents' bed; his bedroll contained Janey. Musical grandchildren. Through the jumble of clothing, bedding, toys, and towels, I searched frantically for the phone. If I didn't turn out that light soon, they'd both be awake. . . . Ah! I lifted a pair of sand-soaked jeans and the phone fell to the floor. Hen turned over, and I dove for the light switch and returned to the porch, blowing sand from the mouthpiece.

Sadd was peering through the screen into the darkness. He said, "Where is that idiot?"

"Looking for the kids, probably. Sometimes they go up to the jetty."

"If he hits that water alone, he's a goner."

"Too bad about him." I was feeling callous and outraged at the spoilation of our last eve-

21

ning together. "The man is not our responsibility." I sat down and gazed at the instrument in my hand. "How does one get an overseas operator?"

But Sadd had opened the screen door and taken a few steps across the sandy stubble. He said over his shoulder, "Responsible or not, we don't need a catastrophe," and trudged farther toward the water.

I struggled through half a dozen informations, exchanges, and operators and finally got the number. I made a mental time check to be sure I wasn't calling in the middle of the night and put the call through to Rachael. Her nice voice said. "Rachael Shea here."

"Rachael!" I cried. Why does one's voice tend to go up an octave when speaking on very long distance? "It's Clara Gamadge!"

"Clara Gam— ? Clara! Darling Clara, where are you? At the Dublin airport? *Say* you're at the Dublin airport!"

"I'm afraid not. I wish I were. I'm in Massachusetts."

"Oh, dear. I mean — that's lovely, of course. The usual cottage in Chatham?"

"Yes."

"That picture you sent at Christmas — you and your grandkids on the beach — was it taken there?"

"Yes, last summer."

"The little one is the image of you." Her voice changed. "Clara, no bad news, I hope." The last time I had phoned her was when my husband died.

"No . . . er . . . actually, we had a rather nice surprise today."

"Did you?" Rachael sounded understandably puzzled as to why she was being phoned in Ireland to be told of a rather nice surprise in Massachusetts.

"Armand is paying us a visit."

"Who?"

"Your brother, Armand."

There was a pause.

"Clara, this is a perfectly good connection, but I'm not getting you. Did you say my brother, Armand?"

"Yes. Out of the blue. I hadn't seen him in years."

Another pause.

"My dear, one of us is cuckoo. My brother Armand is sitting right here next to me doing the crossword. He says not to hang up till he can say hi."

2

Sadd came back through the screen door as Rachael's voice kept hitting my ear.

"Clara? . . . Clara? Are you still there?"

"I'm here." Plain fright drove me to profanity. "Then who the hell is this guy?"

"Wait." She babbled questioningly to someone. Sadd stood looking at my face, then walked into the house, and I heard the receiver in the kitchen lift off. His voice came to me half-real, half-electronically.

"What's up?"

"It isn't Armand," I said.

Rachael was back. "Clara, Armand — the real Armand — wants to know what this person looks like."

"Like you, Rachael," said Sadd. "This is Sadd, my dear."

"Sadd! Is it really you?"

"Yes, but it isn't really Armand, you say. Then who is it?"

"Sadd!" Another voice, another extension,

this one in Ireland. "This is Armand — the *real* Armand."

We all began to giggle nervously, and I said, "We could make a joke about this all being 'real,' but it's too scary. Who *is* this creature?"

Armand said, "Is he still there?"

"Yes and no. He's gone for a swim with the kids, but he'll be back."

There was more offstage murmuring, then Rachael said rather faintly, "Boyd."

"Who?"

"Crazy cousin Boyd," said Armand. "I'm surprised you didn't recognize him, Sadd. That summer at Bar Harbor —"

"Armand, that was sixty years ago. Besides, you Everses all look alike."

"I know. Especially Boyd and me. We were forever being mistaken for each other. Our grandmothers were sisters, you know. Boyd was wildly theatrical. We used to call him the poor man's Orson Welles. I loved the theater myself but gave it up years ago."

I said, "None of this explains why he showed up here today claiming to be you and carrying a lot of family records that he said —" Sadd coughed, and I got the message — "he said he wanted to read to us."

Profound silence. The kind that occurs in the middle of innocuous conversation and proclaims that a nerve has been struck.

Then Armand said, "And did he?"

"Read it? No," I said truthfully. "But he wants to leave it all here so I can —"

"Clara . . ." Armand's voice was brisk. "Let him leave it. Don't bother to look at it — it's nothing but a lot of boring family records. Send it to my home in Grosse Pointe — same old stand on Shaker Street — and I'll be home next week. I think I get the picture, and it's pretty sad. Boyd is trying to find something in there that will entitle him to some money. Twice he tried to break his father's will, and he's probably penniless again. He's borrowed from me countless times. I can only assume he's impersonating me because my reputation is fairly solid and you might have heard that his is not. I'm sorry this happened. I've had such a lovely visit here with Rachael . . ."

He talked on, Rachael making muffled sounds of assent, and I felt increasing frustration. Finally I said, "Okay, Armand, but wait till he gets back here and I face him with —"

"Clara, don't." It was Rachael's voice, suddenly urgent. "Don't even say you called me. Just let him go."

Sadd said, "I agree with you, Rachael. I don't know why, but I agree with you."

"So do I," said Armand.

"Well, I don't." I was baffled and mad.

26

"Why should I let him think he fooled us?"

"Clara, he's crazy." Rachael's voice was pleading. I wanted to say, "No, he isn't, Rachael," but Armand was being brisk again.

"Clara, say *nothing*. Ship all that stuff to me and forget the whole thing."

I was about to raise more objections when my daughter's laugh wafted to me across the dark sand. Blast. They were back. I said, "Rachael, I'll call you from New York."

The sudden burst of terrible, strangled sobbing that came across the wire was worse than anything that had gone before. Sadd's receiver went down quickly, as did Armand's. Stunned, I hesitated, wanting to say something more, something consoling or inquiring but all I could come up with was a feeble, "I'm so sorry, dear," and then pushed the little button that silenced the awful weeping.

Why should a mere shoddy trick — as Armand apparently considered it — cause Rachael such desolation?

I could hear the young people showering in the back. Sadd came out to the porch, slapping at a mosquito. He said, "It comes back to me now. The look-alike Evers cousins, Armand and Boyd. They used to play sophomoric jokes like showing up on dates for each other, the girl not knowing the difference."

Henry padded out to the porch, a towel

around his middle. He cupped his hand to carry his whisper. "Where's that charming guy? Gone, I hope."

I got out of my chair. "You didn't see him on the beach?" Dear God, where was the man?

"No. Was he there?"

"He went looking for you."

"He missed us, fortunately. Let's turn out all the lights. Maybe he'll get lost."

"Mom says she's going to kill somebody." Hen appeared, yawning. "The person who left the screen open in Uncle Sadd's room. Mosquitoes like crazy."

"What!" Sadd marched into the house, and we followed to find Tina and Paula batting about in the tiny bedroom. Andy, still out under the shower, called, "Quit that racket — you'll wake up the kids."

"And *you'll* wake up the neighbors." I went to the kitchen door to shush him. "Doesn't anybody realize it's eleven-thirty?" I walked back to the fray. "The clothes, by the way, belong to our visitor."

"What clothes?" Paula missed a mosquito and knocked over a lamp.

We were all crowded into the room, slashing about with towels and folded newspapers. Janey had staggered awake and was jumping on the bed. I looked around for quasi-Armand's belongings. No clothes, other than

Sadd's, lay or hung in sight.

"He stripped," Sadd said. "We know he did."

"And we saw him on the beach in your suit."

The others had stopped their siege and were staring at us. Tina said, "Are you talking about that awful man?"

"Yes." I went to the window. The old, ill-fitting screen was in place.

Paula said, "It was wide open when we came in. Did the weirdo go out that way?"

"No," I said, "I saw him walk through the hall."

Henry said, "Whoa!" and grabbed Hen and Janey. He looked at me. "I have a feeling we've missed a whole episode here, haven't we?"

I nodded.

Tina moved. "You two" — she drove the kids before her — "into the kitchen for ice cream, then back to bed instantly." She looked over her shoulder. "Consultation on the porch?"

I nodded again, and Paula looked around the room. "I think we've got them all, Sadd."

"If we don't," Sadd said grimly, "you and Andy have a roommate tonight."

Paula went to check on her baby, and Sadd and I went back to the porch. Andy followed, toweling his hair. He said, "What's all the fuss about?"

"About that bad actor who was here."

Andy looked around. "I forgot about him. Where is he?"

"You tell us," said Sadd.

"I don't follow you."

"Andy," I said, "we're barely following ourselves. Wait till the others get here."

He went into the house, and Sadd and I pulled two straight chairs from a corner of the porch and sat bolt upright, looking at each other. The night had cooled off beautifully, but I felt literally hot and bothered. From the kitchen, the sound of voices in debate came to us, then Hen and Janey, giggling and clutched by their fathers' hands, came dashing past us.

"Midnight skinny dip!" called Henry, and for the next five minutes I was happily distracted by the squeals from the water's edge. Then they were being packed back into bed, gasping and gurgling. Their mothers, Sadd, and I sat in the darkness eating ice cream.

"I'll say this for you young people," said Sadd, "you certainly role-switch with the greatest of ease. I don't believe I ever put either of my children to bed."

"Dad did," said Paula. "With wonderful stories."

Yes, I thought with a quick ache, wonderful stories. . . . I said, "But think of all the uplifting things you *did* do for your kids, Sadd. Like sending their letters back from school or camp, blue-penciled and edited."

" 'Blue-penciled and edited' is a redundancy," said Sadd. "And I still do that when they write to me."

Paula hooted and Tina choked on her ice cream. She said, "Remind me to keep in touch with you entirely by phone."

"Speaking of phones" — I picked up the instrument, which still lay under the lamp — "this one has just been in touch with Ireland."

"Ireland!" they echoed as Henry and Andy appeared.

Henry said, "Start from where what's-his-name said his sister Rachael might —" He snapped his fingers. "Rachael — sure — she's your friend in Ireland."

"And she's my godmother — I just remembered!" Paula sat up.

I'd forgotten that myself. "So she is, dear. . . ."

"Well, lay it on us, Mom," said Henry.

I "laid it on them," an expression Sadd considers an abomination, and sensed their startled faces in the semidarkness. When I finished they sat in silence for a minute, then Andy said disgustedly, "Actors! He was having a ball with this impersonation."

Tina said, "What a jerk. Didn't he say he

31

might be murdered? He deserves to be."

"Where do you suppose he is?" Paula dished out more ice cream.

"He never caught up with us on the beach," said Henry.

Sadd said, "He's either floating around out there facedown or sitting in the Hyannis airport in my bathing suit."

"No," I said, "he never went into the water. He threw his clothes out your window and then came back and got dressed. I hope he's on a plane back to New York."

Another silence. Then Henry said, "When you talked to Rachael, what was her reaction to all this? And her brother's? Were they appalled? Scared?"

"No," I said, suddenly realizing that's what they should have been. "They only seemed . . . exasperated. Till the end."

"End of what?"

"The conversation. I had to cut it short because I heard you people coming back and I was afraid he might be with you. I told Rachael I'd call her when I got back to New York, and she went to pieces." I picked up the briefcase and stared at it with utter distaste. "I didn't have the heart to tell them we'd heard all the family scandals. I just said he'd brought the stuff. Armand said it was 'boring family records' that Boyd was trying to work a shakedown from. Armand said to send it all to him and forget it."

"Will you do that?" asked Paula.

"Absolutely. I hate the sight of the thing." I dropped the briefcase to the floor again.

Tina said, "And will you call Rachael like you said you would?"

"*As* you said you would," murmured Sadd, who was nodding on his chair.

"I don't know," I said truthfully. "I've been asking myself the same question. I don't think either of them is anxious to discuss it further."

"Well, I'm going to bed." Sadd stood up. "And all I know is I've lost a bathing suit — unless it's pinned to a bush out back with a thank-you note."

Henry laughed. "Who knows? Let me check."

For some reason — perhaps the same one — nobody else laughed. Sadd stood uncertainly by his chair as Henry put down his dish and went out the screen door. His steps crunched the sand. We sat there, nobody speaking or eating. Perhaps, like myself, they dreaded a sign of the man's existence. I wished desperately I'd never seen or heard from him or, at the very least, never would again.

But Henry was back with the bathing trunks. He took a piece of paper from the half-zipped back pocket.

"I think it's addressed to you, Mom. I can't see too well. . . ." He tipped the light toward him.

I couldn't see too well, either. I said, "Read it, Henry."

He read:

Clara: Don't believe a word they say in Ireland. *He's* Boyd. He's after her money. Please help. I'll call you in New York — if I'm alive.

Armand

3

As that dear, darling man, actor-writer Robert Morley, once said, "Where grandchildren are concerned, it is a mistake to voice one's misgivings out loud."

So I bit my lip, wanting to strangle Hen and Janey, who were tearing around the jam-packed Hyannis airport while their parents harangued me. The harangue had, in fact, begun last night and gone on unabated till this minute.

"Mom, you should *not* go back to New York."

"Why not? I live there. I think Hen just bumped into that toddler who's screaming."

"It's not safe, Clara, with that character on the loose. We're just worried that —"

"Worry about your daughter, Andy. She's about to be run over by that baggage cart."

Tina said, "Suppose somebody actually does murder him and picks your place to do it at?"

"Then isn't the usual procedure to call the police?"

"If you just weren't going home alone."
Henry grabbed his son.

"You're almost next door," I said. He and
Tina lived in Brooklyn Heights and practiced
law in the same firm.

"Your mother is *not* going home alone," said
Sadd. Everybody looked at him, and he looked
back smugly.

"But your flight is to Sarasota," I said.

"It *was* to Sarasota. I changed it. You're
stuck with me for a while."

They all looked relieved. Paula seized her
careening daughter and said, "Well, if you're
sure you won't come back to Boston with
us . . ."

"Darling, thank you, but I've been away
for a month, and I need to get back to that
place there's no place like. So kiss me, everybody, and go home."

I hugged my infant granddaughter, the
other two were collared and told to thank me
for the lovely visit, and they scattered into
the crowd.

Sadd said, "Have you ever heard my im-
itation of Maurice Chevalier?"

"No."

He sang, " 'I'm glad I'm not young anymore.' Would you like a drink?"

"Please."

As we pushed through the pre-Labor Day

36

throng, Sadd said, "I still can't make up my mind if he *is* Armand."

"Neither can I."

"That pair in Ireland. Are they the villains?"

Oh, my poor Rachael — the least likely villain in the world. But certainly there was something out of kilter there. I sank onto a plastic chair in the mobbed lounge, feeling depressed. Sadd gave an order to the beleaguered waitress, then looked at his watch. He said, "We have thirty-five minutes."

"Sadd, this is extraordinarily kind of you."

"A drink? I don't see what's so —"

"You know what I mean."

"Well" — he ate a pretzel — "I'll enjoy a few weeks in New York if you can 'hack me,' as the kids say. That's one bit of slang I rather like. It's bluntly expressive and sounds —"

"I can hack you just fine."

Sadd and I, both single in latter years, had rediscovered our cousinship and the pleasant fact that we hit it off despite dozens of points of difference. One of these points was that he considered Florida — he had moved there on his retirement — to be paradise.

"Besides," he said as our drinks arrived, "Florida can be beastly hot in September."

"I thought Florida was perfect in every respect."

"Oh, come now, I'm not that blind a convert."

Actually, he was. Sadd had fallen in love with the little barrier island of Santa Martina in the Gulf of Mexico and from his home there had written two books, one on the endangered beauties of the state, the other a tirade against developers.

My mind still on Armand — if he *was* Armand — I said, "I know one thing: if that guy surfaces again, he'll have to show me every form of identification known to man. Do you think he will?"

"Show you?"

"Surface."

"Oh, he'll surface all right. When did you say you'd be home?"

"In a few days."

"Your phone could be ringing right now. Do you have an answering machine?"

"No. I hate those things. I'm either home or I'm not."

"Clara, you are almost as reactionary as I am, and that is a ghastly indictment."

I sipped my bourbon, my mind elsewhere. I said, "I'm not sure I want to continue with this, anyway. The whole thing is so screwy."

"We haven't heard the whole thing."

"Rachael is no more illegitimate than I am."

"How do you know?"

"Preposterous."

"Why preposterous?"

I said idiotically, "I knew her mother. She was a lovely woman."

Sadd stared at me. "That is about the nuttiest non sequitur I've ever heard."

"I *hate* to think of it. May I have another drink, please?"

"No, you may not. You'd be on my hands. Clara, your problem is that you are hung up on the word *illegitimate*. Don't you realize it's practically an archaic term as regards children?"

"I realize" — I chewed on some ice to cover the quaver in my voice — "that if Rachael knows it to be so, she's carried the weight of it all her life, and if she doesn't know it and is confronted with it, it could kill her. She's a sensitive woman of our generation, and if that briefcase contains —"

"I forgot about the briefcase." Sadd's glass stopped in midair. "Have you opened it?"

"No."

"Where is it?"

I indicated the shabby brown case leaning against the table leg. The noise in the lounge was deafening. I thought about Rachael. She'd never been beautiful but had been striking, vivacious, and warm. Her marriage had been a disappointment to everyone in the family but her. She had met Steven Shea, a teacher in a Dublin elementary school, while on a European tour in 1938, just before the roof of the world fell in. He was reading his own poetry in a pub, Rachael had told me, and she'd walked up to him and told him he was wonderful. They were married the same week, and she'd never returned to the United States.

Sadd said, his thoughts apparently along the same lines as mine, "Her family wasn't happy about Rachael's Gaelic romance, as I recall."

"No."

"I connect the Everses with banking and boating, none of them particularly interested in literature."

"I doubt if any one of them except Rachael ever read a book for pleasure. That's why Steven Shea was such an embarrassment — a poet yet!"

"Shea!" Sadd put his glass down. "There's a young Irish poet named Herrick Shea writing today."

"It's her grandson. She mentions him often. He's all she has. Her son was killed in a car crash and his wife remarried and lives in England. If I promise not to guzzle it, may I have another bourbon?"

"Too late. Let's go."

At the gate, Sadd stayed with my belongings

and I went into the restroom. I felt wretched. In the last month I'd eaten too much, gotten too much sun, watched too much television. My mind was mush. I poked at my hair, which is long and white and worn, at the sentimental request of my son and daughter, in a pile on the top of my head. Dammit, it was a pain. I'd cut it off and get a frizzy permanent. And I'd take that class in painting at the Academy of Design — I could walk there from my home on Sixty-third Street, and God knows I needed to walk — and maybe I'd take a Berlitz course in Spanish, too, and maybe, just maybe . . . I'd go to Ireland.

Rachael wasn't a villain. She was a victim.

I stared at my image in the mirror, not seeing it. The woman beside me said, Why didn't they have paper towels, she hated these blowers. I agreed, holding my wet hands under an ineffectual blast of warm air. Would I make matters worse for Rachael by going? But she'd seemed genuinely pleased to think I might be calling from the Dublin airport. Should I tell her I was coming or just show up? Usually I hate that — "Yoo-hoo! Look who's here!" — but an unheralded arrival might better reveal her true situation. There were certain risks, of course. Would she be strained? Defensive? There's an immense chasm between a letter in which one can select, shade, omit, and a face-to-face visit with its searching looks, betraying voices, and rampant vibes. I'd stay at a hotel and say a firm "No" to any suggestions that —

Good Lord, was that my flight being squawked? I seized my pocketbook and made for the door. Sadd stood glowering outside.

"I was about to risk arrest by going in after you," he said.

We boarded, and I stowed my carry-on. Did I have everything? Where was that briefcase? Under Sadd's arm. I sank onto my aisle seat. We weren't together, owing to his late reservation, and three rows up he was throwing aloft his raincoat and book bag. Sadd always traveled with a small library; his worst terror, he said, was to find himself stranded somewhere with nothing to read. Now he took off his seersucker jacket. He invariably wore a suit while traveling. "Feckless informality" was destroying our culture. Only since he'd moved to Florida had we been able to persuade him to dispense with a tie.

He folded his jacket and stowed it, then sat down with the briefcase on his lap. The back of his sunburned neck glistened with perspiration. The airport had been freezing, and the plane was comfortable. What ailed him?

The man beside me said, "Would you like your husband to sit here? I'll change."

I thanked him and indicated to my "husband" that we were being done a favor. My seatmate crawled over me, and I moved in — I hate the trapped feeling of the window seat — and Sadd clambered back.

"Are you okay?" I asked.

He propped the briefcase up on his lap and started to unzip it. Then he stopped and said, "Do you remember . . ."

"Do I remember what?"

"Where we were sitting when Armand — if he is Armand — related his story?"

"Of course. On the porch."

"He didn't read any of this, did he?"

"He never even opened that thing. Why?"

Sadd looked at me sideways. He said, "You've forgotten your seat belt. Fasten it — literally and figuratively."

I tugged at the belt, snapped it, grabbed the briefcase, and unzipped it.

It was neatly packed with wads of newspaper.

4

"Clara, can you forgive me?"

"No."

"For Rachael's sake?"

"It's for Rachael's sake I *can't* forgive you."
I rested the receiver on one shoulder and tore
open two packages of instant soup. "But keep
talking and make it good, Armand — if you
are Armand."

"You know I am."

"I do not. Tomato or split pea?"

"What?"

"I'm talking to Sadd." He had just walked
into the kitchen, yawning and trailing his
bathrobe. "He came back to New York with
me yesterday because he thought — and so
did my kids — that I wasn't safe here with
a lunatic like you around."

A groan. "I don't blame them."

Sadd said, "Soup for breakfast?"

"It's the only thing in the house. Call it
brunch — it's almost eleven."

"Tomato."

The voice on the phone said, "When do I get a chance to explain?"

"Right now."

"I'd rather see you."

"You saw me."

"Yes, and I embarrassed you to death."

"You also let a horde of mosquitoes into the cottage."

"What? Oh, God — the window screen! That was truly unforgivable. But I had to get out of there and give you a chance to call Ireland. As soon as I saw you on the phone I split for the airport. I couldn't face you again that night."

"I don't know how you can face me again ever." I reached for the kettle, which had started to whistle.

"Clara" — his voice was pleading — "I realize that what I did was in very bad taste, but when you said your family was there, it gave me an idea. If a whole bunch of people heard the account and knew my life was threatened —"

"Oh, yes, I forgot. You're about to be murdered. May one ask by who?"

"Whom," said Sadd, holding out his mug.

"Go ahead and joke," said the voice. "You can't imagine how desperate Boyd is. He's washed up as an actor, he's broke, and he's got a bad heart. He'd do absolutely anything to get his hands on Rachael's money, which he knows she's leaving to her grandson and to me."

"How do you know that?"

"She told me, and I foolishly told him the last time I saw him. He asked me for money — he was always asking for money — and I told him I was strapped. I'd just put my wife in a nursing home — she's gone with Alzheimer's — and my daughter was in the middle of an expensive divorce. I told him I myself was tempted to borrow from Rachael since she'd been sweet enough to tell me that —"

"Oh, by the way," I interrupted this spiel, "I better send you back that briefcase. Those records made fascinating reading."

Now the voice was sheepish. "I knew Boyd would tell you to send him the stuff, and I wanted him to be shocked and scared."

"It didn't occur to you that *I* might be shocked and scared?"

"I'm sorry. I figured you'd be too disgusted to even open the thing."

"I was. Sadd opened it. We got the shock intended for Boyd — if he is Boyd and you're not."

"Stop saying that. I'm leveling with you, Clara. That bastard has Rachael completely hoodwinked. She hasn't seen him — or me — in ten years, and she's almost blind."

Blind!

The mug jerked in my hand, and soup splashed on the table. Sadd said, mopping it, "Who's blind?"

"Rachael." That settled it. I was going to Ireland.

The voice was saying, "One o'clock tomorrow then? You and Sadd? Here at the Dorrence?"

"What?"

"For lunch. Clara, you're not listening to me."

"I've listened to you long enough, whoever you are. I'm going to Ireland to be with Rachael."

A sharp intake of breath. Then, slowly. "I think I like that. . . . But give me a chance first to tell you more about Boyd's backup plan, namely the question of Rachael's birth. Please come tomorrow. They have a decent dining room here. One o'clock. I'm in room four twelve."

I said, "Armand — and I'm not convinced that you are Armand — if we come, you'd better be ready to show me identification right down to a piece of your baby hair."

It was the first time I'd heard him laugh. "I'll do even better. I'll ask my granddaughter to join us. It just occurred to me — she lives here in New York. You'll like her. She writes poetry."

"I'll like her even better if she's really your granddaughter. I don't trust you. By the way, is Rachael well off?"

"Very well off. You see, Mother went back to Gross Pointe after my father was killed so handily in the war, and she herself only died a few years ago in her nineties. Even though she was never happy about Rachael's marriage, she was fair, and she left everything equally to Rachael and me." For the first time the voice was hesitant. "I pretty much blew my share. Some bad investments. . . . But Rachael did well with hers, and I think her husband came into some money at one point. Yes, Rachael's loaded. I'll tell you more about it at lunch tomorrow."

I hung up and sat staring at the phone. Sadd said, "I gather we're going to see him."

"Tomorrow. Lunch at his hotel. How's the soup?"

"Fine, if you keep saying to yourself, This is brunch. Did I hear you say you're going to Ireland?"

"Yes. Come with me."

"I thought you'd never ask."

Sadd walked to a travel bureau on Third

Avenue where a friend of mine presided. I'd left everything in his hands, only stipulating that the visit not exceed a week; we mustn't look like a rescue party. We would tell Rachael we were stopping over en route somewhere.

I spent the next few hours doing laundry and walking around touching things. One of the great joys of being away is coming home, blowing the dust from favorite photographs, plumping unplumpable sofa cushions, and saluting all one's beloved junk. A not very expensive print of *The Laughing Cavalier* beamed down at me from the top shelf of the bookcase. We'd bought it because Henry Gamadge had always loved the painting and said it was the only way to look at life. I blew it a kiss. Home is where the Holbein is.

I called my friend Sara Orne and asked her to get a replacement for me at bridge that week, then napped, if somewhat fitfully, for most of the afternoon. Oh, the heaven of one's own bed. Did I really want to swap it so soon for seven or eight hours on a transatlantic flight? But Rachael was "almost blind." Why had she never mentioned this? At our age letters tend to recount current ailments, and anything as vital as failing eyesight . . . And why had she wept so suddenly, so convulsively? Perhaps for no sinister reason at all; hadn't I myself sometimes grown weepy at the unexpected sound of an old friend's voice? And prime questions: Was her visitor indeed her brother, Armand, and were Sadd and I having lunch tomorrow with rapacious cousin Boyd?

It was still one man's word against the other's.

At six o'clock Sadd suggested that rather than submit to my cooking he take me out to dinner. We walked up Madison to a favorite spot of mine, a little cellar of a place called Emile's. We stood under the canopy for a few minutes, and I inhaled the soft September smog. I was home.

Sadd said, "In Florida at this moment the egrets are clustered around my lanai, wondering where the hor d'oeuvres are. Did you know that unlike a gull, who eats anything, an egret will only take fish or meat?"

"They deserve to go hungry."

"Oh, no. A creature that beautiful has a right to be picky."

"Well, this creature is neither beautiful nor picky and will eat anything, thank you."

Emile himself gave us a smile and came close to remembering my name. "Nice to see you back, Mrs. er . . . How was Cape Cod?"

"Just lovely. If there's a wait, may I have a glass of Chablis?"

"No wait. The rest of your party is here."

The what?

From the cavernous recesses of the place my son, Henry, appeared, grinning. Sadd said, "Don't blame me. He called while you were napping and set this up. I told him if I'd had my kids in the house for a week, I'd be sick of them, but —"

"But you're you and I'm me and this is lovely, dear." I kissed Henry. "Is Tina here?"

"Yes, she's ordering some bon voyage champagne. Sadd told us about Ireland and Rachael going blind and all."

"Do you think we're crazy? I mean, to go."

"To Ireland? No, that's neat. But I don't much like you going to the Dorrence tomorrow."

We'd arrived at the table, and Tina said, "Just when you thought you'd dumped us. But Henry's worried."

"About what?" I said as we sat down. "The perils of going to lunch at the Dorrence?"

"Yes," said Henry. "I'd like to go with you. I don't trust that guy."

Sadd said, "Henry, there's a small matter of etiquette — he hasn't invited you."

"You know what I mean. I'd eat somewhere else in the room and keep an eye on you and wait for you afterward."

I was very touched and put my hand on my son's. "Thank you, dear, we very much appreciate your concern, but really, what can happen to two elderly persons having dinner in a hotel dining room with a third elderly person? You're just back from vacation, and I'd hate to have you take another day from the office —"

"Tomorrow's Labor Day."

"— as well as the time it would take you to pile all the way back here again."

"Of course," said Sadd, eating celery, "you'd be useful if your mother should get a bowl of poisoned soup intended for our host and collapses. I don't do heavy lifting."

I glared at him over the menu, and Henry said, "Have you fully decided he *is* Armand?"

"No," I said.

"Henry," said Tina, "something just occurred to me: Suppose Armand — or whoever he is — decides to take them someplace else to eat. What could you do?"

"He could hail a hansom cab," said Sadd, "and follow us rapidly through the fog-shrouded streets."

"Okay, okay, forget it. Let's order," said Henry.

I reiterated my thanks, and we concentrated on the menu. When the waiter had departed Tina poured champagne and said, "What kind of identification will you ask for?"

"The usual, of course, license and so forth. Then I'll want the name of the nursing home where his wife is and the address of his daughter, and I'll call both places before we go down for lunch."

"You're going to his room first?" Henry looked alert.

Sadd rolled his eyes. "Shall we drop breadcrumbs in the hall like Hansel and Gretel so we can be traced to his door for rescue?"

"What's the room number?" Henry said doggedly.

"Four twelve," I said.

He wrote it down. "Did you tell him you were going to Ireland?"

"Yes."

"What was his reaction?"

"He said, 'I think I like the idea.' "

Henry grunted. "Not exactly fulsome."

"No. And now I have a question." I sipped my champagne. "I want you to answer one at a time, and think before you do — as Perry Mason would say. Who wants to answer first?"

"Number one son, as Charlie Chan would say."

They looked at me expectantly, and our salad arrived. I said, "No reason not to eat while you think," and dug into my lettuce. I took two bites, then said, "Here's the question. Who is the man in Ireland? Is it Armand or is it Boyd? And if it's Boyd, has Rachael been faking belief because she's frightened, or does she truly believe he's Armand?"

I drained my champagne and buttered a roll. Sadd drenched his salad with blue cheese dressing, and Tina held a pepper grinder over hers. Henry crunched on a cucumber and looked into space. Finally he said, "The man in Ireland is Armand. The man who came to our cottage is Boyd — your lunch date tomorrow."

Sadd shook his head. "It's Boyd in Ireland, but she believes it's Armand."

Tina said, "Both wrong. Yes, the man in Ireland is Boyd, but Rachael's eyes are so bad she can't be absolutely sure and she's terrified."

Our dinner arrived, and I began talking about how good the food was at Emile's. A fourth, startling possibility had just occurred to me.

5

Labor Day. Everybody streaming back from abroad except a pair of crazy old-timers about to stream there.

"Sadd, we must be insane." Twenty-four hours and a good night's sleep had somewhat clarified my vision. "Were the tickets very expensive?"

I folded a sweater and mashed it into what I vowed would be my single piece of luggage. The morning sun streamed through my window, highlighting the antiquity of my bag, which lay, bloated and protesting, on my bed.

Sadd leaned in the door. He said, "What time are we due at the Dorrence for lunch?"

"One o'clock. You've asked me that twice. You're ducking my question. How much were the tickets?"

"Put it this way: Your friend at the agency wangled everything from senior citizen rates to off-season discounts to some coupons she unearthed. Aer Lingus swallowed hard and

55

gave us a break. It's all on my Visa. Pay me when you win the lottery."

"I've never bought a lottery ticket in my life."

"So tough luck for me. Would you have room for this?"

"If it's another book, no." I must have sounded ungracious after his princely gesture regarding the tickets, but *must* Sadd be a walking bookmobile?

"It's very slim — look — nothing to it," he said. "I found it in your bookcase. How can one go to Ireland without something of Yeats?"

"Easy."

But I took the slender volume because Henry Gamadge had loved it and slid it into the once crisply ruffled, now sagging side pocket of my suitcase. How many last-minute items had caused that sag? . . . Once, a nearly forgotten baby's bottle, another time my husband's galleys, just arrived. How could a baggy strip of rayon cause such a flood of memories?

Sadd looked at his watch. He said, "I'll admit to being slightly apprehensive about our timing."

"Why?"

"We'll have to dash from our lunch date with Maybe-Armand — as Tina calls him —

to Kennedy. Can we make it?"

"What time is our plane?"

"Seven. But they want you there in chains hours before."

"I don't see a problem." I slid my suitcase to the floor. "We give Maybe-Armand from one to three, get a cab from the Dorrence, and should be at Kennedy by five." I sank down on the bed. "I'm pooped. Do I have time for a nap?"

"Better just rest and read. A nap will demoralize you."

"How?"

"You'll wake up relaxed and sensible, wishing you'd never thought of this junket and wanting to cancel it."

"I already feel that way."

"I'll bring you a shot of bourbon. It will revive the poison in your system."

Sadd went off, and I lay down on the bedspread, looking out at the acacia tree in my yard. Mostly it hugged the kitchen window, but a few branches reached the bedroom. I thought of one of my favorite poems by Anne Sexton, "Three Green Windows." She'd waked from a nap and lain looking at the crowding luxuriance of suburban trees. My bedroom only had one window and one tree, but it was lovely and brave despite being what Sadd called "city scrawny." Above all, it was honest. Don't be an ass, Clara, a tree can't be honest; it can only be a consolation for dishonesty. What dishonest elements were working against Rachael?

I turned over. What was I getting myself into? How would I explain to her not mentioning this trip when we talked? Should I call her now or when we arrived in Dublin? Then, probably. I'd forgotten to ask Sadd what hotel we were booked into. I'd never been in Dublin, so what did it matter? Would Rachael be glad and cordial? Cool and distant? And her ambiguous houseguest. How would he welcome us?

I sat up and punched the pillow. You're getting too old for this stuff, sister. If my mind was mush before, now it was puree.

Sadd came in with the bourbon as the phone rang. He lifted the receiver, then said, "Certainly, she's right here." He gave me the glass and put his hand over the mouthpiece. "Young, female, hopefully beautiful. No, dammit, that is *not* the right use of 'hopeful.' One hopes, beautiful."

"Hopefully I'll get the phone," I said.

A young female, beautiful or not, said, "Mrs. Gamadge? I'm Armand Evers's granddaughter."

Encouraging! Surely a fake granddaughter wouldn't risk calling unless —

"Grandfather told me you're going to Ireland. May I — that is — I wanted to ask — could I go with you?"

Sadd had wandered off, so I had nobody to register astonishment at. Would three sips of bourbon cause me to be hearing things? No, those were definitely her words: Could I go with you?

I said, "Er . . . I'm so sorry. We — my cousin Mr. Saddlier and I — are leaving tonight."

"Tonight!"

"What a shame. If only I'd known." Known what? That some strange girl wanted to attach herself to me for eight or nine hours? "Yes, I'm afraid we're on an Aer Lingus flight at seven. Will we see you at lunch?"

Click — she was off.

Sadd wandered back. "That didn't take long."

"Sadd, the darnedest thing." I repeated the conversation. "Does that tell us anything?"

"Only that the young lady — whoever she is — isn't one to bore you with chatter."

The phone rang again. Sadd reached for it, said hello, then smiled. "Young, female, *definitely* beautiful. Paula."

My daughter's voice said, "I heard that! Thanks, Sadd! Mom, I had to know: Has that gink showed up?"

I filled her in on "gink" developments and the Ireland trip.

"Clara Gamadge, you're a saint."

"Or an idiot."

"Henry's right, though. Ireland's a great idea, but going to the Dorrence . . . Well, keep your guard up. No use telling you not to go, I suppose. You're as bad as Dad."

"That's the nicest compliment I've ever had."

Her laugh quavered a little. "You know what I mean."

"Of course I do, darling. I'll be okay, and Sadd will be with me."

"Oh, come on — that's like saying Fuzzy Bear will be with you. Anyway, another reason I called" — there was a rattling of paper — "I got thinking about Rachael being my god-mother, so I dug out my baby book and there was this pretty card from her and it says, 'A Quaker blessing.' Is Rachael a Quaker?"

"Now that I think of it, yes." Shocking how facts can slide from one's mind in the course of years. "Her husband was a Quaker, and Rachael became one. She used to write to me about her research into the history of the Quakers in Ireland. Read me the blessing."

" 'Be thou happy, be thou blest, from thy birth until thy rest.' "

"How lovely. Paula, thank you, dear. I'm

so glad you told me. Now I can mention it to Rachael, and I know it will please her."

"I better go. Janey's whacking me and the baby's yelling. Awful day."

"It won't last forever. They grow up." I refrained from adding that then the pain was only different. "And don't worry about your old lady. I'm looking forward to seeing Dublin. My great-grandmother was Irish, you know."

"You never told me that."

"Of course I did. Her name was Bannon. She came from County Sligo, I think."

"Okay, Mother Machree." Paula giggled. "Just take care of yourself."

The Dorrence, on the Upper West Side of New York City, was a commercial hotel that about twenty years ago had managed to excavate enough space inside it for a small swimming pool and now plumped for family trade. The taxi driver gave us this bit of trivia as he put our suitcases on the sidewalk.

Sadd and I stood looking at the slightly grubby facade over which the sign "Swimming Pool" upstaged all else. My memory of recent dips in the blue-green surf at Chatham made the words faintly repellent.

Sadd said, "I hope the food is decent."

I fanned myself futilely with my hand. New

York was still September warm. We went in and checked our bags at the desk. The frigid lobby was the usual violent contrast to the street. Sadd buttoned his jacket, and I was glad I'd brought my silk shawl. We went to the house phone and I rang room 412.

"It's Clara and Sadd, I hope?" said the unmistakable Evers voice. "Thank heaven. Come right up."

Thank heaven? I'd said we'd come, hadn't I? Why so fervent?

Three other persons got out at the fourth floor and headed assuredly down the hall. Sadd and I sought room numbers and arrows.

"Down here."

The voice was Maybe-Armand's, but then it wasn't. The man standing in the door was Maybe-Armand, but then he wasn't. He was an inch or so shorter and slightly balder. He was holding out both hands and smiling.

"You're amazing! I'd know you both anywhere. Boyd should be back shortly. I'm Armand. I just got in from Ireland."

6

He ushered two zombies into the room.

I suppose we said something — at least Sadd must have, because our host laughed and said, Yes, he agreed, jet lag always did seem worse coming from abroad because the darned old sun was lagging, too. Then he said wasn't it typical of Boydie to invite people to lunch and show up late, and how about a glass of wine?

Sadd said that would be nice, and I looked at him with respect. His face wore the slightly blitzed expression that must be all over mine, but at least he could speak. In fact, he was still speaking.

"It's been a long time, Armand. Nice to be back in touch with the Evers family again."

"Darn right, Sadd." Armand — what else could I call him? — turned to an impromptu bar set up on a table and dragged a third chair to it. "But before we say another word — Clara, you've lost a wonderful husband since I last saw you."

"Yes."

"I always said Henry Gamadge was a man in a million."

"Thank you. Harriet died, too, you know."

He transferred his sympathetic look to Sadd. "Sorry to hear that, Sadd. But at least you've been spared what I'm going through. My wife is in a nursing home — mind completely gone." He surveyed the table. "Now, I have Scotch I just got at the duty-free shop in Shannon, if you'd prefer it to wine."

We both said we'd like the wine, and Armand went into the bathroom for another glass. During the three or four seconds he was gone, Sadd and I looked at each other in wordless bafflement. Was he Armand? *Was* he? Now he was back wielding a corkscrew, his tone apologetic.

"You know, this is downright embarrassing, but so typical of Boyd. He was supposed to meet me at Kennedy — in fact, he offered to when I called from Rachael's to say I was coming. He said we could visit here for a day or two before I went on to Grosse Pointe. No Boyd, of course. I got here in a cab about an hour ago and found a note saying you two were coming to lunch and he'd be back shortly."

Armand had poured wine into three plastic

glasses, and now he laughed and asked how we liked his Waterford crystal. He gave us each a glass and raised his.

"Well, here's to cousin Boydie — predictably unpredictable cousin Boydie."

We sat down and I said, "Armand, why did you say 'Thank heaven' when we called from the lobby?"

He crossed his legs and looked into his glass. "Because, Clara, if he had to be late, I was grateful you and Sadd got here first. It gives me a chance to discuss something with you. Frankly, I'm not just irritated with Boyd, I'm worried. I really think he's headed for a breakdown. That business of showing up at your cottage and pretending to be me was the last straw. Oh, we all know he's forever the actor, but there are limits. I simply don't know what he expected to achieve." He took a sip of his wine. "Well, yes, I guess I do know, and I think I told you on the phone the night you called Rachael."

Armand recrossed his legs and swallowed more of his wine. "I don't know if you ever met Boyd's father, my uncle, Bishop Evers. Delightful gentleman — much loved and admired. He left most of his money to charity, which enraged Boyd, but the old gent knew his wife's money would all go to Boyd, and it was plenty. Of course Boyd blew it in no time with his nutty theatrical enterprises, and now he's trying to break some of those charitable endowments his father set up."

Armand's voice was strained and his face rather white. He went on, "The whole thing has kind of ganged up on Rachael and me lately, and that's why I went to Ireland to see her. After your phone call she was distraught. She asked me to come back here and keep an eye on Boyd, which I'll be glad to do" — he cast a wrathful look at the door — "if he'll just show up!"

I literally didn't know what to say, and again Sadd came to the rescue. He accepted more wine with the comment, "These family tangles can be ghastly, especially if the persons involved were close once. Wasn't Boyd more like a brother to you growing up?"

"Absolutely." Armand sat forward on his chair. "He and Rachael and I were raised together — our grandmothers were sisters — and Boyd and I have this freaky resemblance. People were always mistaking us for each other, and sometimes it was fun. We once appeared as the twins in *The Corsican Brothers*. That was when I was still fooling around with ideas of a theatrical career, but I discovered I didn't have what it takes. I went into a brokerage firm, and I'm retired now." Armand's eyes went to the window. "There were some great times growing up, which is why I hate to see Boyd disintegrating. Clara, more wine?"

"Thanks."

"By the way, I hope you sent all that stuff he gave you to my Grosse Pointe address." He poured, looking at me anxiously.

I thought the safest thing to say was, "I didn't want to touch it. I told him to take it with him."

"Good for you. Now" — Armand settled back in his chair — "I've relieved my mind just by talking about it, and thanks for the ear. Enough. I want to hear about you two. Sadd, I understand you've retired to Florida. How do you like it?"

I knew Sadd could digress happily and indefinitely on that subject, so I excused myself and went into the bathroom. I leaned against the wall and closed my eyes.

Where was Maybe-Armand — or Boyd, as I now grimly began to think he must be. Was I a shade disappointed? Had I been subconsciously rooting for him to be Armand all along? Why hadn't he shown up? What had tipped the scales? My going to Ireland? His cousin's sudden return? He hadn't even risked going to the airport. Second thoughts must have told him the meeting would be stormy. I tried to follow his reasoning at the end . . . just leave word that Clara and Sadd were

67

expected and vamoose.

I soaked a face cloth in cold water and held it to my eyes. I wished I could get out of lunch. I wanted only to go to Ireland and console and confer with Rachael. I was sick of the look-alike Evers cousins and this charade. As I went back into the room Sadd was saying, "It's called *Saving Our Shores*. It was published a few years ago, but I still get mail from all over Florida. I've become a rather rabid environmentalist."

"We need more like you." Armand stood up. "I think we should eat. No reason to wait for our delinquent host. If he shows up, fine. If he doesn't, you'll be my guests."

Sadd said absolutely no, and they wrangled politely. Armand went to the phone between the beds and asked for the dining room.

What happened next is a blur because it came so fast.

Sadd stood up and took my arm. He said, "Clara, come look at this. It will bring back memories."

He propelled me to the window, which looked out on a vista of roofs, yards, and distant Hudson River wharfs. Leaning over my shoulder, he pointed elaborately.

"Remember February 1944, the *Normandie* lying there on her side? I think I can even pick out the exact slip. . . ." His finger waved before my eyes, and he whispered, "I don't think he's Armand. I think he's Boyd."

The voice behind us was asking about reservations. Had there been one made for Evers? There had? For how many? I got out a gasping whisper: "What makes you think so?"

"Will you ever forget that day?" Sadd continued nostalgically. "I was working in the Fred French building, and we all went up to the roof when the radio started those bulletins." A whisper: "Something he said while you were in the bathroom." Aloud: "And people started streaming up to the pier."

"Henry and I among them," I said mechanically. "And they wouldn't let us past the police cordon." I felt suddenly a little elated. "And we just had to stand there and watch her burn." In a whisper: "What did he say?"

Our host was explaining that there would be only three persons in the party instead of four.

Sadd whispered, "I asked him if his granddaughter was going to join us for lunch and he said, 'Granddaughter? I don't have a granddaughter.' " Then aloud: "And all they could do was just pour tons of water into her till the poor, beautiful thing just keeled over."

Behind us: "But if the fourth member of the party does show up — it will be a Mr. Boyd Evers — tell him we'll be right down."

My whisper: "Then where's our man?"

Sadd's whisper: "I don't know, and I'm worried." Aloud: "I loved that ship. Harriet and I crossed on her three times."

My whisper, as the phone receiver went down: "It isn't conclusive, but don't tell him we're going to Ireland." Aloud: "Wasn't it years before they righted the *Normandie*?"

"Yes, it was," said Boyd — my God, *was* he Boyd? — joining us at the window. "And when they towed her down the river every vessel saluted her as she passed. Very poignant. Where did they take her? I can't remember."

"To New Jersey to be scrapped," said Sadd.

"Awful. . . ." Boyd put a hand on my shoulder and Sadd's. "They're expecting us. At least Boydie did make a reservation, so let's hope he'll join us eventually. Clara, don't forget your shawl." He lifted it from the bed. "What a beauty."

"Henry bought it for me in Mexico. It always makes me feel like an extra in *The Mark of Zorro*."

Boyd laughed and we walked to the door. Sadd said, "Shall we leave him a note?"

"I don't see why." Boyd looked impatient. "He'll know where to look for us."

"I'm worried about him," I said. "Suppose he doesn't show up?"

70

"He has to. His belongings are still here."
Boyd waved toward the closet. "Come on, let's
forget Boydie and enjoy lunch."

He ushered us out the door and down the
hall, talking a blue streak. "You know, I have
the typical outlander's attitude toward New
York City. I'm appalled by it, but there are
so many extraordinary things . . ." And on
and on, as we entered the elevator, as we left
it, as we threaded our way down the crowded
corridor to the dining room. I was feeling a
little giddy, either because of the wine or because of the hand on my arm of this man who
was probably Boyd Evers.

Our table was a center one in a perfectly
nice if not elegant dining room. I looked
around, half hoping to see Maybe-Armand —
I still thought of him by our wry nickname
— waiting for us, ready to stroll up and con-
front cousin Boyd. But as my glance swept the
room I recognized only Henry Gamadge, Jr.,
seated at a table near the door, absorbed in
a magazine and his lunch.

Oh, darling boy! Oh, true son of your father!
You sensed skullduggery, and despite our
scoffing you came! He looked up as he turned
a page, glanced at our trio absently, then returned to eating and reading. Had Sadd seen
him? I couldn't be sure. Boyd was holding
a chair for me, which put Sadd with his back

to Henry. Had Henry, with his one glance, taken in the fact that our host was not the man who had come to the cottage? I doubted it; the resemblance was remarkable and the dining room dim. How far into lunch need we get before I could excuse myself, walk past Henry's table, wait for him in the hall, and fall on his neck?

Boyd was ordering drinks. I became apologetic.

"Just lunch for me, Armand. The truth is I have a cold coming on, and I'm going to ask you to let me eat and run."

"Clara's been miserable all morning," Sadd said loyally. "I should get her home pronto."

Henry's waiter was proffering the dessert menu. How long had the poor dear been here? We'd been delayed upstairs, of course, while Boyd digressed — eerily, it now seemed — on his own shortcomings. Brave Henry, who never ate dessert, was pointing to something on the menu; he was going to hang in as long as he could. I had a sudden inspiration. I sat forward, staring across the room.

"I believe I see someone I know — a young man who was a protégé of my husband's. I can't think of his name. Sadd, you may remember him — he's at the table near the door."

Sadd looked over his shoulder, then turned back and drank some water quickly. "Yes.

Promising young lawyer, isn't he? I can't think of his name either."

"Shall we ask him to join us?" Boyd said politely.

"Oh, mercy, no." Mustn't let this backfire. "I'll just run over and speak to him. Order the club sandwich for me, please."

I dodged around our approaching waiter and made for Henry's table.

"Pardon me, but haven't we met somewhere? You look very familiar. My name is Clara Gamadge."

"And that is the oldest pickup routine on earth, lady, but sit down anyway." Henry half stood up and indicated the chair across from him. As I perched on it, he said, "It isn't the same guy."

"How did you know?"

"He's shorter."

"You're a wonder. I can feel your father beaming down upon you from above. We're pretty sure it's Boyd. He's just back from Ireland, still claiming to be Armand."

Henry sipped his coffee. "Where's Armand, then?"

"He hasn't shown." I had a sudden, unaccountably sinking feeling.

Henry's dessert arrived, and he stared in dismay at the large éclair. He said, "Please eat this."

"I haven't had lunch yet. Besides, I hardly know you. Doggie bag it for Hen. I should get back. Will you wait for us?"

"Of course. I'll be in the bar." We both stood up. "It was a good try, lady, but you're a bit old for me."

I nodded at him brightly and went back to an excellent club sandwich and more of Boyd's chatter. I finally interrupted it to ask about Rachael.

"Oh, she's wonderful. Been managing all by herself till lately, when her eyes began to go. Now she has a companion. The house is one of those big, lovely old ones in Herbert Park. She keeps very active, especially in her church. Did you know she's a Quaker?"

"I seem to recall it, yes."

"I'm ashamed I haven't been over to see her before this, but Muriel's decline into Alzheimer's has been so long and appalling. . . . I wish I'd gone to see Rachael when her son was killed, but I didn't. She has a grandson, a young man who's devoted to her. He teaches at Trinity and writes poetry. His name is Herrick."

The waiter hovered, and Boyd took out his wallet and extracted his credit card. He laid it on the table, groping for a pen.

The name on the card was plain: ARMAND EVERS.

My throat began to close. I remembered how it felt to be on the end of Crack the Whip. One more crack and I'd land in the stands.

It was at this moment that the disturbance in the hall started.

7

It was a murmur at first, then a low babble. Heads on the waiting line in the hall turned, and necks craned in the dining room. The babble took on the higher pitch of questioning. "What's happened? What's the matter? What? What . . . ?"

Sadd was putting cash on the table for the tip, and Boyd was insisting it was all on his card and put your money away; their argument died as the sounds grew. I got up and started toward the door with some other people. They hurried, I walked slowly, my heart leaden. I claim no gift of prescience, but leaden it was. Henry was among the neck craners in the hall. Now Sadd and Boyd were beside me. The sound of an ambulance siren reached us.

Sadd said, "Anybody know what's wrong?"

I shook my head. Boyd said, "I'll reconnoiter," and started out.

Sadd said, "Do you want me to go, too?"

and again I shook my head — it seemed to be my one capability — and sat down on a chair at an empty table near the door. I sat for three reasons: it would be madness to push into that crowd, I dreaded finding out what was wrong, and my knees were shaking. I picked up a glass of water from the table and took two swallows, unconscious till a minute later, of the insanely unsanitary act; I just needed water. Sadd, looking horrified, took the glass from my hand.

I said, "Did you see his credit card?"

"No."

"It said ARMAND EVERS."

"He stole it from him."

Our eyes turned toward the hall where two policemen moved about in the crowd. Please disperse, folks. There was an accident, but only one person was involved, it was all taken care of, and kindly clear the hall.

A woman's voice, callous and laughing, said, "Probably some old geezer had a heart attack in the lobby."

People began to filter back into the dining room. I caught snatches:

"Jeez, what a ghastly thing."

"I'm glad I had my lunch."

"The management will freak out."

"How could that happen? Where's their security?"

Sadd put out his hand and touched the arm of a man as he passed us. He said, "Excuse me — what was it?"

"Some guy drowned in the hotel pool."

He moved on, and we looked after him vacantly. Sadd said, "Now, Clara, it isn't necessarily . . ."

"No," I said, "it isn't necessarily . . ."

"Shall I try and find Henry?"

"Please."

He stood up, but Henry was coming toward us with his father's slightly loping stride, magazine hugged under one arm, a glass of brandy in each hand. He said, "I want you to drink this. It's him."

We stared at him, and he went on, "I'm not going to tell you another thing till you've each had two sips." I obediently took two sips, and Sadd drained half of his. Henry sat down beside us.

"The identification — his clothes were on the edge of the pool — says he's Boyd Evers. The pool was closed pending cleaning. He could have sneaked in for a swim and had a seizure or just plain decided to end it all. They think the former. His distraught cousin, Armand Evers, is confirming the identification."

I felt numb. "He said Boyd would kill him, and he has."

"Probably," said Henry. "Do you want to wait for Boyd or split now?"

"Split now." I stood up. "I can't face that murderer and his phony grief."

"Clara, wait a minute." Sadd was frowning. "Sit down and finish your brandy. We have to think."

"If I finish that, it will finish me," I said rather wildly. "He'll be back any minute. I want out of here."

"Sure you do, Mom, but Sadd's right — we have to decide on a scenario. Boyd has to still think you think he's Armand."

"Why?"

"Because he's a killer, that's why."

But I was beside myself. I said, "You two figure it out. I'm going — by way of the kitchen — because if I met that man in the hall, I'd go old-fashioned bonkers. I'll walk around the block to the lobby, and if I'm not mugged before I get there, you can tell me your scenario on the way to the airport."

I made for the swinging door to the kitchen and went through it. I went up to a white-haired woman who was slicing celery and said, "I need the bathroom and I can't get through that crowd in the lobby. Is there one —"

"Oh, sure." An elderly person with a hurry call needs only another elderly person to be understood. She led me down a tiled hall and knocked on a door.

"It's empty." She pushed the door open for me.

"Thanks so much."

"Terrible, isn't it — the man that drowned."

"Terrible."

I locked the door and stood in the cramped, grubby room, staring at the wall. A sign over the toilet read "Wash Your Hands."

Good advice, Clara. Wash your hands of the whole thing. Don't go to Ireland, go home. Call Sara back and tell her you'll be there for bridge on Wednesday. Tomorrow start the painting class at the institute. *Wash your hands.*

Then I pictured Rachael picking up the phone and getting Boyd's sorrowful report. Would she know it was her brother who was dead? Had she ever believed . . . And I was sickeningly back at square one.

I opened the door and peered down the hall toward the kitchen entrance. I reached it, pushed open the door, and confronted the covered stretcher being carried from the freight elevator to a van.

Oh, dear God. . . . I leaned against a dumpster and felt sick. I heard Paula's laughing voice:

"Oh, neat. The story wouldn't be complete without a murder. Whose?"

"Mine."

80

Some of the kitchen staff had gathered in the court. They glanced at me, and I had a fleeting vision of the strange sight I must make leaning against a dumpster in my Spanish shawl, gagging. But then in New York there is no such thing as a strange sight; I was just another drunk old broad.

I said, "How do I get to the front of the hotel?"

One of them pointed and said, "Left, then a left at the corner, then another left."

I went blindly. The van passed me as I turned the first corner. I looked at my watch. Three-thirty. Enough time, but the zero hour for crawling toward Kennedy was approaching. I hoped Sadd would remember that our suitcases were being held at the main desk. Nothing could induce me to walk in there and chance coming face to face with Boyd. I walked faster. The air felt good. Rounding the second corner, I could see the hotel marquee and the big "Swimming Pool" sign. Cringe. Now I slowed down, keeping a wary eye on the entrance. Henry and Sadd emerged with our two suitcases and carry-ons. I waved mightily, and they came toward me.

"About-face, Mom. My car's in a garage down that way. How do you feel?"

"I'm okay. Did you see Boyd?"

"No, we deliberately avoided him. I have

a plan — tell you about it on the way."

Sadd said, puffing, "Must we sprint? This bag weighs a ton. I know, I know — it's the books — but we have plenty of time."

"Well, not plenty, but enough," said Henry. "You two wait in this deli." He guided us toward the brightly lit entrance. "I'll get the car."

He set our cases beside a window table and took off. Sadd and I sank down and pushed dirty dishes away. I pulled off my shawl and stuffed it into my carry-on.

Sadd said, "This simply is not happening. We're going to wake up in that cottage in Chatham and compare notes on the same dream, like Peter Ibbetson and Mimsy."

A waitress came to clear the table and asked what we wanted. We said coffee and sat in exhausted silence till it came. Then Sadd said, "I'm trying to follow Boyd's thoughts as he searches high and low for us. What will he do when he can't find us?"

"Call my house."

"And when he gets no answer either tonight or tomorrow?"

"I don't know."

"Will he phone Rachael with the bad news?"

"I'm afraid he will. I'd give anything to be able to break it to her, but . . ."

"Who will he say has drowned?"

"Boyd, of course. He's solidly locked into the Armand impersonation now."

"He must be absolutely desperate for money."

"He is. Remember when Maybe-Armand told us —" I bit my tongue. The derisive little title had slipped out.

Sadd said, "I wonder if he has any concept of what it takes to carry off this type of impersonation. A lot more than just stealing credit cards. Not only does the family have to buy it —"

"He's lucky," I said. "Armand has only the wife who's out of it and the daughter with the 'expensive' divorce. But who is she? Where is she? And if the divorce was expensive enough, she might have been persuaded to play ball with Boyd."

"There's the granddaughter. Boyd didn't know about her."

"Unfortunately, neither do we. She never showed. And she might be the one person who could identify him. If Boyd can wrap it all up before she checks back with Grandpa, she'll never find him." I stared out of the window at the traffic. "Actually, he might get away with it. You may be sure he's looked into every angle."

Sadd pushed his coffee away and leaned his

elbows on the table. "Well, if all it takes to get Rachael's money is this impersonation, why the big deal about her parentage?"

I said, "Armand was going to tell me about that, but I think I can figure it out. . . . If the impersonation didn't work, Boyd could always threaten to 'expose' her doubtful origin."

"But if Rachael should give him the classic 'Publish and be damned' — which she very well might — who would there be to scandalize? The poet grandson? I can almost hear him laughing."

"I rather think he has her Quaker friends in mind. Embarrassing disclosures. . . ." I sipped the coffee I didn't want. "I have to keep reminding you, Sadd, that the stigma of illegitimacy is still very real to women of our generation. Poor Clementine Churchill dreaded the revelation of it all her life. At least the press waited till after she was dead." Sadd said nothing, and I added, "I wonder how he did it."

"Who? What?"

"Boyd. The drowning."

"Drugged him, probably, Henry said. He also said there should be an autopsy."

"Who would order it — the family? Boyd hasn't got one. He never married. There's only his grief-stricken cousin Armand, but

84

somehow I doubt — There's Henry."

We left enough money on the table and got our bags to the street. Henry, double-parked, got out and grabbed them, then hustled us into the car. He headed for the East Side.

"Dear boy," I said, leaning back, "have you any idea what you have done for us by coming today?"

"I keep remembering how extremely gracious I was when you proposed it," said Sadd. "Let me now apologize and say 'Thank you.'"

"All part of the Gamadge service." Henry winked at me in the rearview mirror. "But it's important to talk now. This is all the time we'll have to discuss the thing."

The traffic was heavy, the day darkening. Henry negotiated the streets as only a born New Yorker can. He said, "We don't want Boyd to smell a rat when he can't find you. Sadd said you didn't tell him you were going to Ireland."

"No."

"Then it will be an absolutely spur-of-the-moment, madly spontaneous decision when you learned the drowned man was Boyd."

"How did we learn it?" I asked.

"From me. You remember me — your husband's protégé whom you spoke to in the dining room? You saw me in the hall when the hubbub started. You were anxious, you were expecting a friend, would I ascertain the identity of the dead man? I did so. Shocked and horrified, you took off for Kennedy at once, on a condolence mission to your girlhood friend, the dead man's cousin. You asked me to let your son, a *brilliant* lawyer in Brooklyn, know, and requested that he call Armand Evers at the Dorrence Hotel in the morning and explain."

" 'Brilliant' is the word," Sadd said admiringly.

I said, "Will he buy it, Henry?"

"I think so. And be enormously relieved not to have to see you again."

"How long will he stay at the hotel?"

"As long as he's officially needed, I'd guess. Then all he has to do is throw Armand's ashes down the toilet and continue with the game plan."

I said, feeling queasy again, "Don't talk till we get to the expressway. Then I have a few more things to ask."

"And I have a few more things to add," Henry said.

"And I wish I'd gone back to Florida," said Sadd.

We jounced along, and I tried to empty my mind of everything but Rachael. Please, God, let her be glad to see me. She had a companion,

Boyd had said; yes, she'd mentioned the companion in recent letters. How had I forgotten that? Would the companion like me? What difference would it make? Oh, a lot, a lot. The companion could be one of those jealous, possessive creatures who hovered and influenced. Influenced what? Really, Clara, you're in your dotage. Things hardly made sense anymore.

"One day," I said.

"What?" my companions said together.

"For visiting Rachael. We'll spend *one day* with her. It will just be a condolence call. What else can we do in Dublin the rest of the week?"

"Oh, lots of things." Sadd brightened. "There's the National Museum, marvelous bookstores —"

"Yes, one day." I realized I was repeating myself.

"What's your problem, Mom?" Henry had all his father's sensitivity.

We were on the expressway, making fairly good time. It was cloudy and chilly. I rolled up the window beside me and made myself say the words aloud.

"I'm suddenly worried to death that Rachael will tell me to mind my own business."

"So you will," said Sadd. "And come home. No harm done."

"Except by the man who murdered her brother."

"Not your concern," said Henry.

"Murder is everyone's concern. I quote Henry Gamadge."

"Look, Mom —" An enormous truck passed us, drowning his words. He waited till it was gone, then said, "Here's what I wanted to add: Try to get some element of pleasure out of this jaunt — even if it's just the sense that you're doing a pretty neat thing."

"Sadd's doing the neat thing," I said. "He's treating."

"Yeah, Sadd!" Henry grinned at him approvingly. "Let me assure you both that Rachael will be overjoyed to see you. Boyd's phone call will have left her prostrate no matter who she thinks has died. I'll phone you after I've talked to Boyd — Shit! I've *got* to remember to call him Armand. Mom, write down Rachael's phone number or address or whatever you've got for her."

I fished in my pocketbook for a pen and something to write on. What was this? A paper napkin, Hotel Dorrence. I shuddered and scribbled Rachael's address on it. We rode the rest of the way in silence, and Sadd went to sleep.

At Kennedy Henry dragged our bags to the pavement, kissed me, and vanished. We stood amid the din and throng till all was processed, then jostled into the mainstream and reached the security point. As we stood waiting to heave our carry-ons onto the conveyor belt, Sadd said, "What time is it?"

"Five. We'll find the gate and sleep. I could do it standing up."

"Me too."

I unzipped my carry-on and pulled out my raincoat. The attendant said, "Are you going to wear that, ma'am? If not, put it on the belt."

I threw it after my pocketbook, and we walked through to reclaim the gear. Sadd said, "What's the raincoat for?"

"A pillow. If I fold it like this —"

"Mrs. Gamadge?"

A very young voice. I turned to see a tall, attractive girl with long dark hair, great bangs falling into her eyes. She wore jeans and a sweatshirt with the words *Gerard Manley Hopkins Lives.* She was looking at me with a sort of anxious eagerness.

"Yes?" I said.

"I'm so glad I found you! I'm Armand Evers's granddaughter."

8

I said stupidly, "Oh?"

People pushed past us, and the girl went on excitedly, "I'm sorry I couldn't make lunch, but the minute you said you were on this flight I called Aer Lingus and it wasn't full and I'm *on!* I'll be paying for it forever, but it's worth it. I'm actually going to meet Herrick Shea! Oh — I should have told you — my name is Vee. V-e-e. How's Grandfather?"

Most of this outburst was a blur, but the last sentence hit like a thunderbolt. I opened my mouth and out came, "This is my cousin, Charles Saddlier."

Sadd smiled, held out his hand, and said, " 'I caught this morning morning's minion, kingdom of daylight's dauphin, dapple-dawn-drawn —' "

She flew at him and kissed him. "You're the first — the very *first!* I made it myself — I do silk screening — I wear it all the time,

90

and you're the first!"

Sadd, quite pink with pleasure, spouted on, " 'Of the rolling level underneath him steady air, and striding High there . . .' "

What was this insanity? Was he trying for another kiss? And at what point should I break in with something like "Sorry to interrupt, but your grandfather was murdered today." Now she was chiming in and they finished together.

" 'Fall, gall themselves, and gash gold-vermilion'!"

Sadd smiled at me rather condescendingly. "Gerard Manley Hopkins, English Jesuit poet, 1844 to —"

"Five-thirty," I snapped. "We should find our gate."

"It's number eight," said Vee, gamboling ahead of us. "I left my duffel there and came back here to wait for you. I've been sneaking peeks at baggage tags, and Grandfather described you, so it was easy."

Grandfather again. Dismay engulfed me. Sadd, recovering from the kiss and the poetic flow, looked equally unhappy. I said, "Vee, this is a delightful surprise, but we're both pretty exhausted. It's been a long day for old-timers like us, and I'd planned to rest, even catch a nap before the flight. I never can sleep on planes."

"Neither can I." She looked sympathetic, then elated. "So we'll have the whole flight to talk!"

Oh, joy.

Sadd came valiantly to the rescue. He hoisted his carry-on to his shoulder and reached for mine. "We've had a very strenuous day, my dear, so before another word we must find the restrooms, have a drink, and get a seat to deposit our old bones in."

"I'll deposit my bones, too." Vee laughed. "I'm pooped."

She looked about as pooped as a hummingbird. Then she pointed. "There's a bar over there — Oh, it's one of those stand-up deals. You don't want that. Why don't you guys go ahead to the gate and get a seat and I'll bring you something."

We guys looked at each other. I asked in surprise, "Are you twenty-one?"

"Last week. What'll you have? I don't drink."

"Two bourbons," said Sadd, taking out a bill. "And whatever you'd like yourself."

She nodded and darted off. We trudged on, exchanging dismal looks. Sadd said, "When will you tell her?"

"*I?* When will *I* tell her? I think you'd better do it — in blank verse, maybe."

"Clara, we can't hit the girl with it now.

She's too happy. Besides, what could she do?"

"Be the only one to identify her grand-father."

"Sure. And be introduced to the pool at the Dorrence by Uncle Boydie."

That sobered me. "Well, we can't let the whole flight go by — let alone the whole week — without telling her. Dammit!" I suddenly felt put upon beyond endurance. "I don't need this kind of aggravation!"

We parted at the restrooms, and I fumed and stewed and moaned till I rejoined Sadd, who immediately said, "How about this: To-ward the end of the flight we tell her about Armand — just the sad news of the drowning — nothing about murder."

It sounded so acceptable that I walked an-other ten steps before realizing its flaw. Then I stopped.

"Sadd, according to everybody but you and me and Henry, it's *Boyd* who's dead. Armand lives. Like Gerard Manley Hopkins."

He looked at me in despair. "I wish you wouldn't be so blasted analytical. It comes from spending all those years with Henry Gamadge. So she's got to be told all or noth-ing?"

I nodded. We were pushing through the crowd surrounding the gate. Seats looked scarce. We started down a full row. I said,

"I wonder how fond of Armand she is — was — whatever. If Boyd never heard of her, they can't have been close."

"And how did she ever hear of Herrick Shea?" said Sadd.

"She writes poetry herself, Armand said. But is Herrick that well-known?"

"No. At least, not in this country. But there's a whole underground world of poets. They know each other's work, who's good, who's not, who's been published, who hasn't, they know the pecking order for grants and fellowships, and they're all madly competitive and insanely jealous of each other."

I saw a man beginning to gather up his gear and quickened my steps. I said, "This girl doesn't sound jealous. More hero-worshiping."

"Which makes her very vulnerable. Don't ask me why, but poets are catnip to women. Does Shea know she's coming?"

"How should I know — nor do I want to." I dove for the empty seat as the man cleared it. "I'm not really up for an eight-hour exchange of confidences. Let's hope she's at the other end of the plane."

"If the flight isn't full, there's no escaping her." Sadd looked around. "Clever of you to find that seat. Do you see another?"

"Oh, someone will move presently," said

caring Clara. "Just keep circulating."

Sadd stood and stared at a seat across from me that contained a very small boy. Reluctantly his mother dragged him onto her lap.

"Thank you so much," said Sadd. "Would he like a mint?"

"No," said the child.

I was trying to position my folded raincoat between my neck and the back of the seat, but in my innermost weary soul I knew it would not stay put. As it slid to the floor Vee's voice said, "Let me do it. Hold these."

I took the two plastic glasses from her, and she rolled the coat tight and small. "Now try it."

It was as good as it was going to get, and I smiled at her gratefully and handed back one glass.

"Where's Mr. Saddlier?"

I pointed, and she turned and gave Sadd the other. "And here's your change. Thanks for the Coke. I'll be over here."

"Over here" was a corner where a shabby duffel reposed with a number of other shabby duffels. Young people were lying on the floor everywhere. Vee plopped down, pulled her bag under her head, turned on her side, and stretched luxuriously.

I looked at her, consumed with envy.

★ ★ ★

Sadd was right, there was no escape; the plane was half-empty.

Vee sat patiently on her seat six rows up all through dinner, then through our two rounds of cribbage, and now she was looking imploringly back at me down the darkened aisle. I looked at my as yet unadjusted watch. Midnight. Sadd was dozing. It would be cruel to delay further. I got up and worked my way up the aisle. We transferred to an empty six across row.

"This is wonderful," Vee breathed. "I'm so happy to be here with you, Mrs. Gamadge. Grandfather said I'd like you, and I do!"

Quick — steer the conversation away from Grandfather. I said, "Tell me your last name. And does 'Vee' have any significance?"

"Don't laugh — it's really Verity. My mother loved Restoration novels and named me for one of the heroines. Pretty silly, so I made it Vee. My last name is Loftus. My dad married Armand Evers's daughter right after her divorce last year, so I picked up a grandfather. I only met Armand once — at their wedding — but he was so nice and said to call him Grandfather, and I love it because I never had one. He asked me for my address and sent me money at Christmas."

Relief! A stepgranddaughter who'd only met Armand once! Even so, it would be a shocking revelation, and I shrank from it. I said, "How do you happen to be familiar with the work of Herrick Shea?"

"Oh, Mrs. Gamadge, he's only one of the most incredibly great poets of the century. Of course, he's only been published in Ireland, but that will change, you'll see. I have both his books. And his grandmother is a friend of yours, Grandfather said. What a break for me!"

"Why?"

"Well, it's just that — I mean, it will look more like —"

"Vee," I said, "does this incredibly great poet know you're coming?"

A subsiding of eager posture, a fingering of magazine in the pocket of the seat ahead. "Yes, in a way. . . ."

In a way. The words were a knell. "I mean, when you look him up, will it come as a surprise to him?"

"Not exactly. I've given him plenty of warning."

Warning. Worse and worse.

Vee felt in the pocket of her jeans and pulled out a wad of crumpled paper. She separated it carefully. "Here's his answer to my first letter."

I dug in my own pocket for my glasses, snapped on the ray of light that illuminated my seat, and read:

Dear Vee Loftus:

What a charming name! Is it really Vee, or was it once Vera, or Veronica, or Victoria?

You were most kind to write me such a — how shall I put it? — such a *glowing* letter. It is pleasant enough to be told that someone likes my poetry, but when that someone is as articulate as yourself, the praise is doubly welcome.

But forgive me for doubting you when you say I am "much admired in the States." Surely this is a delightful fiction invented by your kind self. Recognition has barely begun in my own country and must be almost nonexistent in yours.

However, thank you for your fine, encouraging words!

Faithfully
Herrick Shea

Courteous. Kind. I couldn't fault him.
"And here's his second letter."
Alas — conspicuous absence of exclamation points. I said, "Had you written him between these two?"
"Yes, a few times. Maybe — five . . . or six."

The letter read:

Dear Vee:

I was, of course, happy to learn that you may visit Ireland for the purpose of doing research. Yes, I can sympathize with anyone coming to a strange country and knowing no one there or, as you put it, "almost no one." I'm honored that you consider you know me "through my poetry."

By all means get in touch with me when you arrive. If my schedule permits, I will try to show you some of the hospitality for which Ireland is famous.

Faithfully,
Herrick Shea

I laid the letters in my lap and tried to think what I would say to my own daughter or granddaughter. No matter how blunt or reactionary I might sound, I hoped my words would carry the element of concern that I felt for this very nice girl.

"Vee, I'm afraid you're chasing this man."

"Yes, I suppose I am."

"How do you know he's not married?"

"The jacket of his last book of poems says

he lives 'in bachelor quarters at Trinity College, where he teaches.' "

"That doesn't mean a darn thing."

"I know."

Wretched silence. I needn't worry about disclosing the death of an elderly man she hardly knew. Possibly much worse pain lay in store.

She took the letters from my lap and said, "I've been wanting to come for ages, but I didn't want it to look like I'd just come to see him. That's why I mentioned the research. And now being with you is so great because it can look like a family trip — you know, his grandmother and all."

Family indeed. Where was this girl's mother? I didn't much want to know the answers, but I felt I should ask the questions.

"Oh, my mom's dead. Dad and Sharon live in El Paso."

"Sharon is Armand's daughter?"

"Yes. So how is that sweet guy? How was lunch?"

"In a minute. You live in New York?"

"Right. I graduated from Hunter last June. I work in a day care center downtown near where I live." A little laugh. "And I try to write poetry."

"Do you like your job?"

"Oh, sure. I get along with little kids."

"And you're on vacation?"

A nod. "I had some time coming and I put it off. Now I'm glad I did."

"How long do you have?"

"Two weeks. My ticket to Ireland is for ten days."

Ten days. Armand would be ashes, and she'd be safe from Boyd.

I said, "Where will you stay in Dublin?"

"I don't know. I'll find someplace." She leaned back with a blissful sigh. "I'm trying to imagine how he looks . . . like Dylan Thomas, I'll bet. . . . Did I tell you I know most of his poems by heart?"

As an Irish friend of mine says in moments of stress, Jesus, Mary, and Joseph. Our whispered conversation had stopped. The drone of the plane, an occasional snore, the rustle of magazine pages under pinpoints of light, were the only sounds.

I suddenly felt cold. I whispered, "Vee, will you see if you can snag me a blanket? I think I'll —"

But she was asleep, dark hair all over her face. Dreaming of her poet, no doubt.

Jesus, Mary, and Joseph with a vengeance.

9

Slants of light through the windows, smell of coffee, hot, damp towels refreshing faces. We were coming down for "a brief lay-over" at Shannon.

I took the moist benediction from my eyes to see Sadd standing in the aisle, looking down at Vee, still asleep, her head heavily on my shoulder.

He said, "Have you told her?"

"No."

"Good. But, Lord, when?"

"I don't know." I'm always irritable in the morning, and this morning I was irritable in spades. I said, moving my shoulder slightly, "Vee . . ."

She jerked awake. "Oh, gosh! You should have dumped me into the aisle."

Sadd said, "Morning's at seven, and all that."

I got up. "We'll be in shortly. Let's agree to meet at customs."

"What? Oh — yes. Sure. Okay." She was still groggy, still probably in the arms of Herrick Shea. I started down the aisle after Sadd. Why had I said that about customs? Why hadn't I said, "Here's his grandmother's phone number. Let's meet for lunch one day."

Sadd said, as we reached our seats, "Where's she staying?"

"She doesn't know, doesn't care, and she's sure she'll find someplace, etc. Why don't we just get lost at customs and head for the hotel. What's the name of it?"

"The Gresham. I was thinking of renting a car."

"Oh?" I concealed my panic. Sadd's driving on a quiet, side road in the country at an off hour is scary enough. The thought of him in a foreign car on the left side of the road, finding his way into Dublin, made me weak. "Why don't we get a cab? It will be quicker."

"Well, if you prefer. And we can give her a lift."

"A lift to where? Sadd, the girl is not our responsibility."

"Of course she is. She's made herself that, and you're too much of a softie to shake her."

I was furious because I knew it was true. I said, "Okay. I'll give her Rachael's phone number." The plane lifted, and I snapped my seat belt savagely. "Right now I intend to go

103

to the hotel and sleep. I may not even call Rachael myself till tomorrow."

"So you give her Rachael's number . . ." Sadd began counting on his fingers. "So she calls Rachael before you do, so Rachael has just heard from, quote, Armand, and hits Vee with it, so Vee's stunned — why hadn't we said something? — so she tells Rachael we're here, so Rachael is floored, and so we look — and feel — shitty."

"Shitty" did it. Sadd seldom uses vulgarisms, and when he does it means he's upset and probably on target.

I said wearily, "After we go through customs we'll get coffee someplace and I'll tell her the whole thing."

The dreary drag through customs took the usual hour or so. Vee was nowhere to be seen. It occurred to me that she may have decided to take off on her own. Why be tied to two old fogies when Herrick Shea might be waiting to give her that royal Irish welcome? We were lugging our bags toward the airport entrance when she caught up with us breathlessly.

"He'll be here any minute! He told me to wait at the coffee shop — there it is! — and I said he'd know me because I'd be holding a book of his poems!"

She was clutching it. I said, with dread in

my heart, "You phoned him?"

"I sure did. I said to myself, No time like the present, and he was just leaving his room to go to the library and he said he'd come pick me up — his voice is marvelous — but he can't hang out with me too long today because he has a class at eleven, and he's bringing a friend with him — please stay and meet them, you two — and the friend's name is Liam O'Coyle. Aren't Irish names neat?"

Neat. Bringing a friend. Safety in numbers? Was it a case of Get it over quick, give her a whirlwind welcome, then try and find me? I hoped not, but I was suspicious of this instant availability. We made our way to the designated spot, I feeling like the designated wet blanket. Sadd said as Vee surged ahead of us, "We're about to meet the Revered One?"

I said, "Don't you think it's odd that he's willing to drop everything?"

"I'm just worried about his dropping *her* after he's rushed her for a few days."

I stood still in the pushing crowd and laughed. " 'Rushed'! I haven't heard that expression since Aunt Robby used it about her debutante days!"

"Would you prefer 'seduced and abandoned'?"

"I'd prefer to get a cab to the hotel this minute, but I haven't the heart. And he *is*

Rachael's grandson."

"Which says nothing whatever about his character."

Vee beckoned to us, and we joined her at the jammed entrance to the coffee shop. She said, "I'm just going to stand here so he can see me better. Can you find a place to sit down?"

We said we didn't mind standing for a bit after sitting all night, and Sadd added, "Better hold that book high, Vee. Do you know what he looks like?"

"No idea."

I said, "But we're hoping for Dylan Thomas with just a dash of Brendon Behan."

And ten minutes later that exact combination came striding through the crowd toward us. Enormously tall, thick black curly hair, baggy tweeds, craggy face, and terrible teeth.

"Welcome to Ireland! I'm Herrick Shea." He put his hands on Vee's shoulders. "And this is Vee of the lovely letters! I want you to meet my friend, Liam O'Coyle." A shorter, red-haired young man with a round face and a nice smile stood beside him. "If, indeed, a man's editor and severest critic can be termed 'a friend' and there are those who cry 'Impossible!' " He drew Vee's hand through his arm. "Now, let us scram from this Circus Maximus and be on our —"

106

"Herrick" — Vee had been gazing and gasping and smiling — "these are my friends, Mrs. Gamadge and Mr. Saddlier from New York. Mrs. Gamadge knows your grandmother."

Herrick beamed on us, but his friend's face changed suddenly. He said as they shook hands with us, "Hirk, I meant to tell you. Your grandmother called last night while I was waiting for you. She said she'd call back and it's important."

Herrick waved this aside. "Mrs. Gamadge and Mr. Saddlier from New York, welcome! Liam, be a good lad and rescue Vee's bag, which is about to be kicked out of sight." His friend and Vee dove after the duffel, and Herrick turned back to us politely.

"And what brings you to Ireland, my friends?"

"Death, actually," I said, "though I prefer you not mention it to Vee. I'm sure that's what your grandmother's call was about."

"Death?" He looked startled. "How unfortunate."

Liam was back with the duffel, and Vee was again gazing up at Herrick with Nancy Regan eyes. He clapped his hands.

"Off we go! Liam and I are at your service for" — he looked at his watch — "one hour and twelve minutes, then it's back to work for both of us. The car is perhaps a ten-minute

107

walk. So where are we bound?"

"The Gresham Hotel," I said. "Vee's staying with us."

She looked at me quickly and gratefully. "Well, for tonight, anyway."

We began to move, Herrick sweeping Vee ahead of us. She carried her own duffel. His hand was on her elbow, the other gesticulating jauntily. Sadd had both carry-ons, and Liam bore both bags. At one point he called to Vee's back, "I like your sweatshirt. He's a favorite of mine."

She glanced back at him with a careless smile.

The hour and twelve minutes that Herrick Shea so benignly bestowed on us was a revelation. The car, it developed, was Liam's. Herrick had only a "darlin' beast of a broken-down motorbike." At his suggestion, we stopped en route for a "darlin' bite and a beer," which turned into a full-course dinner for Herrick. The pub was across the street from the Gate Theatre, and I wanted to ask about that historic spot, but Herrick talked, a ceaseless, flowery palaver, the entire time. Sadd and I kept our eyes pretty much on our plates, so it was hard to tell how this was affecting Vee. Sadd was allowed to pick up the check, and Liam left the tip. We proceeded down broad and busy O'Connell Street to the Gresham.

"Thank you, Liam," I said as they deposited our bags on the pavement, and Herrick assured Vee that he would call her very soon and "whisk her away for a darlin' picnic on a fairy green." They drove off with Herrick waving, blowing kisses, and shouting something unintelligible except for repeated darlin's.

Vee stood still, looking away from us up the street. I put my arm around her, and Sadd said cheerfully, "Quite a colorful guy."

Vee said, "He's a buffoon. And a moocher. And a bore."

"Vee," I said as a porter picked up our bags and we followed him into the hotel, "maybe he was just showing off a little."

"A *little!*"

"Maybe he was just excited at seeing you. He'll probably calm down next time."

"Be less of a stage Irishman," said Sadd.

"Be less of an ass," said Vee.

We stood at the desk, and I registered a second occupant for my room. Vee said, with an expression that tore my heart, "I just can't put him together with his poetry."

"Vee," said Sadd as we started toward the elevator, "it's what so often happens when one meets one's idols. A very risky thing to do. Look" — he reached for her duffel — "give me that thing and go out right now and start enjoying this exciting city."

I could have hugged him. "Darn right! Wander around, get lost, come back when you feel like it — before dark, please — and if we're not here, the key will be at the desk. Room three eleven. Scoot!"

She kissed us both, said, "If it weren't for you two guys . . ." backed away, and disappeared.

We got into the elevator and Sadd said, "Do you think he can redeem himself?"

"No. I think he's either a fully certified bore or . . ." The elevator door opened, and we walked down the hall to room 311. I put my key in the lock.

"Or?" said Sadd, proceeding to the next room and inserting his own key.

"Or" — I pushed my door open and stood still, looking in — "or this is an act to make himself look like a fool and get rid of her."

Our bags were being pushed down the hall. I liked my airy room and walked to the window to look out at the city. Sadd appeared at the door with a flask.

"Sherry?"

"Love it. And something else bothers me."

"Oh, Lord. Let me get some of this in me before I hear it."

Sadd went into the bathroom for glasses, and I had a sudden, sickening recollection of

110

Boyd doing the same. I said as we sat down, "What did you think of Herrick's reply when I said we were here because of a death?"

"I don't remember it."

"And then I said his grandmother's call had probably been about that death, and he said, 'How unfortunate.' "

"So?"

"So, surely the logical reply would have been, '*Whose* death?' "

10

"Mrs. Shea's residence." An elderly, very American voice.

I said, "May I please speak to Mrs. Shea?"

"Could I take a message? She isn't very well today."

I'll bet she isn't, poor thing. "I'm so sorry, and I think I know the reason. I'm calling because of it. This is her friend, Clara Gamadge."

"Oh — Mrs. Gamadge! Yes, of course — she'll want to speak to you. One moment."

Companion? Sounded nice. I gazed out the window at the roofs of Dublin, now glistening with rain. It was four o'clock. I'd been resting and reading and battling jet lag and reluctance all afternoon. Finally I'd picked up the phone. I looked at the empty bed beside me. Where was Vee?

A thump — had Rachael dropped the phone? — then a quavering voice, not at all like her brisk one, and a torrent of words.

"Oh, Clara, oh, Clara! He said you and Sadd were there when it happened!"

"Yes, darling, we were there, and now we're here."

"Here?" Faint, bewildered.

"In Dublin. We decided to come over and be with you."

"You're . . . in Dublin?"

"At the Gresham. Can we come at once so I can give you a big hug and tell you how sorry —"

The sudden sobs were reminiscent of the ones that had sounded in the phone four days ago, except that they were interspersed now with gasping phrases like "You came!" and "You're here!" and "I'm going to see you!"

"You sure are. How long will it take us to get to your house in a cab?"

"No — absolutely not!" That stopped the sobs. "You will not take a cab. Annette will come for you. She was just going home anyway, and she'll bring you here first. Annette, they're at the Gresham."

"Rachael, there's no need —"

"She'll be there in twenty minutes or so, depending on the traffic. Be waiting out front. Watch for a gray Mercedes."

"Is Annette your companion?"

"Yes, and she's a dear."

113

"See you shortly, then."

"Oh, Clara!"

As I hung up there was a knock on the door, and Sadd put his head in. He looked around the room and said, "Where's Dierdre of the Sorrows?"

"God knows." I got off the bed. "I hope she hasn't thrown herself in the Liffey. Did you sleep at all?"

"No. I was reading *Il Penseroso*. It put me in an appropriately somber mood for our mission. Have you called Rachael?"

"Yes, just now." I went to the mirror and started to do something futile to my hair.

"Had she heard from Boyd?"

"Yes, but she didn't mention his name or Armand's. It was all pronouns. 'He' said you and Sadd were with 'him' when 'it' happened."

"Is she glad we came?"

"Overjoyed — just as Henry predicted. Did you bring a raincoat?"

"Yes." Sadd walked to the window.

"We're being picked up shortly by Rachael's companion, who sounds like an American. I hope to heaven she's learned to drive in Dublin. Look at that street!"

I had joined him, and we looked down at the tangle of traffic. Sadd murmured, "What a great city. I studied at Trinity one summer."

He leaned forward. "You can almost see the general post office from here. Did you know it's one of the most famous buildings in the world? It's where they made their headquarters when —"

"Better get your raincoat," I said.

Sadd went back to his room, and I scribbled a note with Rachael's phone number on it, took my own raincoat from the closet, and met Sadd in the hall. As we went down in the elevator, he said, "What do we do about Vee?"

"What I promised: leave the key at the desk."

"She still doesn't know about Armand, does she?"

"No."

We were silent till we'd pushed through the crowd in the lobby and stood on the pavement under my rather ineffectual little travel umbrella. I said, "We're looking for a gray Mercedes."

Sadd buttoned his raincoat. "Do you plan to give Rachael the story straight?"

"Yes. She's got to get it all now. I hope to God she realizes it's her brother who's dead. It'll make it easier for us."

"That won't be the worst part of the blow, of course."

"I know." There was going to be no easy

way to say, "And Boyd killed him."

In the swirling twilight mist O'Connell Street was a sea of headlights. I hoped Companion wasn't cursing us. Annette. A name you don't often hear today. Pretty, though. Sadd turned and faced me.

"I've been thinking of what you said about Herrick Shea. What relation would Armand be to him?"

"Well . . ." I wrestled with chronology. "His great-uncle. His grandmother's brother."

"Not exactly near and dear."

"No. We can assume that Herrick will not be prostrate with grief over Rachael's news. My question is: Will it *be* news?"

Sadd frowned. "Now, Clara, that guy may be a show-off —"

"Sadd, that guy may *not* be a show-off. That guy may be putting on an act."

"Yes, to mislead Vee —"

"Or us. I've been thinking of that possible 'act' all afternoon. The madly fey poet who couldn't be suspected of anything sordid."

Sadd turned up his collar. "I shouldn't have left you alone to brood. You've been imagining all sorts of sinister, farfetched —"

"Listen to me, Sadd." Traffic roared and people hustled by, so I addressed myself to his right ear, the better of the two. "Herrick Shea could have supposed he was his grandmother's sole heir. Then he finds out that Armand was cut in for a considerable amount. So he goes along with Boyd's impersonation on the promise of a bigger share. Not impossible."

Having said my piece, I went back to thinking about Vee. I almost wished she were with us. I wouldn't have to go through this awful business twice. I could sit Rachael and Vee both down and say in Vee's lingo, "Look, you two guys, your brother — and your step-granddad — is dead, murdered by his cousin. We're all involved, so let's put our heads together and work it out." Yes, I definitely wished Vee were with us.

And suddenly — she was!

She came running down the darkening street toward us, wet and laughing and clutching a huge shopping bag.

"I had the most wonderful time! I walked all over! And that Powers Court Centre — the shops! I got all this stuff for the kids in my center." She stopped. "Are you going someplace?"

"Yes, and you're going with us!" I hugged her, soaking my front. "Vee, you're a good sport and I'm proud of you."

She laughed. "The heck with Herrick Shea. And I *still* like his poetry."

Sadd said, "Allow me to make an official

117

pronouncement: I love you."

"Oh, thank you, Mr. Saddlier. That makes it easier for me to ask if I can borrow some money. I saw the most wonderful book —"

"Loans later," I said as Sadd pulled out his wallet. "Vee, fly up to the room — the key's at the desk — and get out of Gerard Manley Hopkins and into somebody dry. We're being picked up any minute."

"Where are we going?" She was backing toward the door of the hotel, bumping into people with the shopping bag.

"To see my friend Rachael, Herrick's grandmother."

"You're sure you want me along?" More backing and bumping.

"Sure!" I called.

"Give me five minutes!"

"Make it three!"

"Time me!"

She vanished. Sadd and I looked at each other almost happily. I said, "How young do you have to be to make that kind of recovery?"

"Very young." He smiled out at the shining wet street. "And, of course, it helps to have discovered a very old — and beautiful — city on the same day."

I said glumly, "And now I have to throw a damper on it all."

"Regarding this full recital you plan to

make" — Sadd wiped the moisture from his chin — "what about the companion?"

"She isn't live-in. She's on her way home. Here she is, I bet."

A gray car had coasted to a stop beside a taxi, and a small, wiry old woman laid on the horn. An Amazon couldn't have produced a louder blare.

"Mrs. Gamadge!"

I waved and called, "One more passenger! Be here any minute!"

"Hope so!" Annette glared at the taxi driver and said something I didn't catch. He subsided. Vee came tearing out of the hotel, struggling into another sweatshirt, which also bore some words. I didn't try to decipher them but grabbed her hand, and we all piled into the car and started introducing ourselves.

"No need," said our tiny driver, "you're Mr. Saddlier, and you're a young lady from New York — Mrs. Shea just talked to her grandson. I'm Annette Pine."

"And I'm starving." Vee laughed. "Could we stop somewhere and get a —"

"Supper's waiting." Annette pulled into the traffic with amazing deftness. "I always get it ready for Mrs. Shea before I leave, so I just defrosted three more steaks. By the way, I'm mightily glad you're here. Poor Mrs. Shea's in a bad way."

Vee looked startled, and I said hastily, "Yes, we heard the news. Could we wait to discuss it?" I caught Annette's eye in the rearview mirror and jerked my head toward Vee. Annette nodded.

"First visit to Dublin for any of you?"

"For Vee and myself," I said. "Mr. Saddlier has been everywhere in the world ten times."

"Mrs. Gamadge is given to exaggeration," said Sadd. "Only five."

Vee said, "What news? Why is Mrs. Shea in a bad way?"

Annette handled it better than I could. "We'll let her tell you, dear. A death in the family. Very unexpected. She just heard yesterday."

"Oh, dear." Vee looked at me. "Should I really be here?"

I patted her hand; might as well begin to break it. "Actually, Vee, it's why we're in Dublin."

She looked bewildered but said nothing. I leaned over and read aloud the words on her sweatshirt. They were printed on a tombstone.

If only I could have managed to be
Born in a tree and buried at sea,
My spirit would hover between and free
And earth would have known no part of
* me.*

Now it was my turn to look bewildered. Vee smiled ruefully. "It's part of one of his poems."

I groaned inwardly, feeling surrounded by disappointment and death. I looked out at the wet streets, wanting to enjoy what I could of this city. Annette, though she needed cushions to reach the wheel, drove with absolute certainty.

Sadd said, "My compliments. You're a great navigator."

"Thanks. I love to drive. And this is a great car. I'd never even been in a Mercedes. It was rough getting used to this left-is-right stuff, but once you do, Dublin isn't much worse than Portland."

"Portland?"

"Maine. Where I grew up."

I said, "How long have you been with Mrs. Shea?"

"Almost a year. Her cousin, Mr. Boyd Evers, recommended me."

If a rock had fallen through the roof I couldn't have been more startled. I saw Sadd stiffen, half turn to look at me, then give it up.

Vee said, leaning forward, "I'm mad about this city. Where are we now, Mrs. Pine?"

"Just Annette, dear. Well, we've come over the O'Connell Bridge and passed Trinity College, and now we're on Baggot Street and in a minute you'll see the U.S. embassy . . . .

Annette continued her comments and Vee asked questions, and neither appeared to notice that Sadd and I sat in silence. I longed to ask Annette how and when she had met Boyd but felt the ice was too thin. Better wait and learn it from Rachael — if, indeed, Rachael knew!

"And here we are. This is Herbert Park."

We had turned onto a wide street bordered by some of the most elegant houses I'd ever seen, most of them Georgian beauties, their long, lighted windows gleaming through the near dark and the mist. Front doors of pink and puce and gold shone under their lights. Annette turned into a driveway, and I saw Rachael's tall frame in a window. It vanished, and her front door opened simultaneously with our car doors. I waved and Annette called to Rachael, "Don't you dare come out — you'll catch your death. Good night, all. See you tomorrow."

We thanked her, and she backed to the street. Then, as we started across the lawn to the front door: "Mrs. Gamadge!"

I turned. The car was standing still, headlights piercing the mist. I walked back to it. Annette was leaning out of the window. She said, looking up at me steadily, "She knows it's her brother who's dead."

I stood there with a feeling of absolute trust in this woman.

I said, "That may not be the worst of it."

"She knows that, too. The murdering rat. He never fooled us for one minute."

And she drove away.

11

We sat with drinks before the fire in the delightful, long, book-lined living room in the kind of accord — even contentment — that can surface in the midst of tragedy when one aspect of it is relieved — in this case, doubt.

Only Vee was shocked and silent. Rachael, haggard but handsome in a beautiful lavender wool suit, sat beside the stunned girl on the sofa as she wound up her story.

"I'm not 'nearly blind' by a long shot. Oh, my eyes aren't what they used to be, but whose are? I hadn't seen either of them in years, and when Boyd called from the airport and said he was Armand, why shouldn't I believe it? They always sounded alike and looked alike. Aren't genes weird?"

I said, "I have a friend who says she can't tell her nephew's voice from her son's on the phone."

"I believe it." Rachael looked anxiously at Vee's stricken face, moved closer to her, and took her hand. She went on, "Well, he arrived, and I had no immediate doubts. I went to bed that night and woke up suddenly, thinking, My God — he's Boyd! I was scared to death. I didn't know why he was doing this. Was he crazy? I thought I'd better play along. I found a pair of Steven's thick glasses — his eyes were *really* gone at the end, poor dear — and said I should be wearing them all the time. I think Boyd felt safer, too. He told me his troubles, Armand's, of course, the wife in the nursing home, and so forth, and said how grateful he was that I'd told him he was in my will. That gave me a turn, and he laughed real quick and said, Of course he hoped he wouldn't see *that* money for a long time. It was all so puzzling and frightening, and I began to think he must be desperate enough to do anything. Now we know he was."

Vee sat forward, her eyes on the rug. Rachael said with utmost compassion, "You poor, poor kid. And you so looked forward to coming to Dublin. Herrick said you were charming."

I thought grimly that just a few days ago the words would have sounded like the bells of paradise. Now Vee scarcely seemed to hear them. She said, her head between her hands, "Are you *sure?* Are you sure you're sure about all this?"

I said, "We haven't a shred of real evidence."

Vee looked up. "But Sharon — my stepmother. Wouldn't she spot him? I mean, he can't fool Armand's own daughter."

Sadd said, "He can if he's careful not to go near her. Where does she live?"

"El Paso."

"Easy. My daughter lives in Toronto. Terrible trip. Can't expect an old man, etc. All he has to do is dodge visits from her, and if their paths *should* cross, and she fingers him, well, there are some very effective threats. . . . I imagine Boyd can be a great threatener."

The chill of these words kept us silent. I refrained from voicing the theory that the daughter might be in on the scam; Vee was stricken enough. And we really hadn't looked into the true abyss: Rachael's possible fate at this man's hands.

She stood up now and said, "Let's come back to it after supper. Sadd, I don't think you ever read any of my husband's poetry. I want Vee to see it, too. Why don't you two explore the bookcase and Clara will help me."

Having deployed her forces, Rachael took my hand and we went down a long hall to the kitchen. There she immediately turned to me.

"Clara, is that girl safe?"

"I think so. Boyd doesn't even know she exists."

We stood looking at each other, then hugged again, and Rachael started to cry. The brave soul shook in my arms.

"Oh, Clara, it was so awful. When you called that night I was almost at the end of my rope. As soon as we hung up he burst out, 'That Boyd! He should be shot! Impersonating me because he knows I'm in your will. I wouldn't be surprised if he tried to kill me — he's that desperate.' I just couldn't stop crying, and he went into a big consolation act and said I wasn't to worry, that he'd go back to New York and maybe give Boyd some money, though he could hardly afford it, so of course I wrote a check —"

"Rachael!" I yanked a chair from the kitchen table and dropped onto it. "You gave him money!"

"It was only a few thousand. Of course I knew it would go right into his pocket, but I had to pretend. I was absolutely terrified of him."

"Give me a drink!" I looked around wildly. "I don't care if it's cooking sherry!"

"I have some nice wine." Rachael laughed a little, to my relief. "I've been saving it for a special occasion, and oh, is this special!"

She took two glasses from the cupboard. "I

haven't been this happy since the day he arrived."

I said, "How long had he been here when I called?"

"A few weeks. And one day Armand — my poor, dear, real brother Armand — called. I was at church. Annette answered the phone."

Annette. Did Rachael know . . . ? But Armand first.

"Where was he calling from?" I asked.

"Grosse Pointe. Mother left him the house there, you know. I guess it's tumbling down. Anyway, Annette said I wasn't home but that my brother Armand was visiting and would he like to talk to him. I guess Armand hung up fast."

Now was the time. I said, "Rachael, what do you know about Annette?"

To my astonishment, she clapped her hands, laughed, then reached for her wineglass and held it up.

"Dear, wonderful Annie! That's where Boyd — pardon my French, as we used to say — really screwed himself. Clara, you'll never believe who she is!"

The phone rang. Rachael took the receiver from the wall, said hello, then beamed at me.

"It's your son calling from New York! Henry, your mother is right here, and she's being an angel of mercy. Do you know anything about this awful . . . You do know. . . . Henry! You were there, *too?*"

I rose and took the receiver from her. The ring must have been heard in the living room because Sadd appeared in the door. He accepted a glass of wine from Rachael, and they both sat down at the table and looked at me as I listened. And listened. Then I said, "Thank you, dear. Thanks ever so much. I'll be back in touch. And, you were so right." I smiled at Rachael. "She's glad we came."

"Glad?" cried Rachael. "Thrilled and grateful describes it better."

I hung up, trying to separate what Henry had told me from my curiosity about Annette. I sat down and picked up my wine.

"It looks as though Boyd may have pulled it off. So far, anyway. Henry talked to him this morning."

"Remembering to call him Armand, I trust," said Sadd.

Rachael nodded. "I had the same problem — had to keep reminding myself to call him Armand."

"He was still in what he described as a state of 'absolute shock,' although he had an 'underlying feeling' of relief that poor, tortured cousin Boydie was at peace at last."

"Bastard!" Rachael cried healthfully.

"The body has been certified as that of Boyd

Evers, death accidental. His grieving cousin Armand will claim the ashes and take them back to Grosse Pointe to be buried in the garden of his own home there. This will be done when said grieving cousin returns to said home to *sell* it."

Rachael gasped. "He wouldn't dare!"

"Of course he would," said Sadd. "That's instant money."

I went on, "He thinks it was wonderful of Sadd and me to hurry right over here and help ease the shock for poor Rachael. He himself will probably do quite a bit of traveling —"

"Ha!" said Sadd.

"— after he has removed his wife from that too expensive nursing home and into —"

"A fleabag," from Rachael.

"— someplace he can better afford. He will also, of course" — my voice seemed to slow of its own accord here — "try to return to Ireland to visit his beloved sister as soon as possible."

Rachael covered her face with her hands, and we sat in silence. Vee appeared in the door. She said, "I think you should contact my stepmother right this minute. She's the only one who can nail him."

Rachael got up quickly. "Come and sit down, dear." She drew Vee to the table and poured a glass of wine. Vee said thank you but didn't touch it. The steaks lay on a platter before us. I stared at the floor and Sadd at the ceiling. The element of rapport we'd established on arrival was still there, but now shot through with outrage and frustration.

"You're right, Vee," I said, "she probably could nail him, but think of the time involved: first, to get in touch with her and try to make it all clear — this is a complicated business to hit somebody with out of the blue and over the phone — and secondly . . ." I stopped.

"I think I know what secondly is," said Vee.

I hoped she didn't, but I had to say, "What, dear?"

"Sharon may be in it with him."

We sat in uncomfortable silence. Sadd said, "That's pretty farfetched."

"Oh, I don't know." Vee stood up. "She loves money. She and Dad fight about it a lot. That's why I stay in New York." She looked at the steaks. "I'm not really hungry, thanks. I think I'll go back and read."

Vee wandered out of the kitchen. Rachael said, "What a darling girl. Herrick was quite taken with her. I don't wonder. I wish he'd get married."

I smiled, thinking that even disaster can't squelch the matchmaking instinct in all of us. I said, "Rachael, who is Annette?"

Sadd said, surprised, "Apropos of what?"

Rachael said, "Oh, yes — I started to tell you." She picked up the steaks and went to the stove. She took a bottle from the shelf and sprinkled something on them.

"She's my half sister."

12

Rachael lit the broiler and slid the steaks into the old-fashioned gas oven, saying, "Don't let me forget them." She took a head of lettuce from the refrigerator and started to separate the leaves as she spoke.

"My family has enough skeletons to fill three closets. I was born in France during the First World War when my mother and my uncle Boyd — now, he was a *saint* — were there trying to deal with one of the worst of those skeletons. My father's illegitimate daughter and I were born a week apart, a month after he was killed at Château-Thierry. Will plain oil-and-vinegar dressing be all right?"

Sadd and I nodded, and I was back on the porch at Chatham, watching Armand's cigar glow in the dark.

"My mother was a rather remarkable woman for her time. She went to see the girl — I believe she was a waitress in the casino at Monte Carlo — and took me with her. She gave her money and our address in Grosse Pointe, and said if the girl ever needed anything, she was to let my mother know. It seems, however, there was a boyfriend who was going to marry her, so things looked reasonably good."

Rachael turned and leaned against the counter, smiling at us. "Can you picture that scene? The two women, each holding one of my father's daughters, discussing practical matters as little Rachael and little Annette looked at each other from their mothers' laps. Oh, the steaks!"

Rachael reached for a pot holder, pulled open the oven door, and the steaks sizzled invitingly.

I asked, "And did she ever get in touch with your mother or ask for more?"

"No, as it turned out, things went rather well for Hélène — I think her name was. Her husband prospered after the war. He opened a café in Nice. He died when Annette was in her teens, and she and her mother came to Portland, Maine, to live with her mother's sister. Annette married but never had children. She'd been a widow about five years when Boyd found her."

The name seemed to silence the three of us. Rachael put the steaks in the middle of the table and pointed to a drawer. I took cutlery from it, and we sat down. Rachael said, "Let's say grace."

We bowed our heads and she murmured something, then began to cry again. I grabbed her hand, dismayed at her shattered condition, and said, "Darling, *don't,* things will be okay now," and Sadd started to eat very fast, saying between bites that the whole thing was intolerable and he didn't know how she'd held up as well as she had.

"I'm an idiot." Rachael wiped her eyes. "I guess I'm just so relieved to see you both, even though poor Armand . . ." She gazed at me in distress. "I suppose they'll just cremate him and that's the end of it, isn't it?"

"Don't think about it," I said. "Please eat. You probably haven't had a decent meal since the phone call."

"No. But let me finish about Annette." Rachael poured the rest of the wine into our glasses and ate a morsel of steak. Then she put her fork down.

"Boyd" — she seemed to force herself to say the name — "was always an operator. That was his real talent. And he was jealous and manipulative and had a 'king-size ego,' as Armand put it. In fact" — she nibbled her salad — "this impersonation he thinks he's carrying off is just the sort of role he might have dreamed of." Rachael pushed her chair back. "That poor child Vee must eat something."

"I'll fetch her." I got up and went down the hall to the living room. The fire was in embers, and Vee was sound asleep on a big chair, *The Poems of Steven Shea* between her fingers. I took the book from her gently, and she stirred and murmured something. I put a sofa cushion under her head, and she settled onto it. I went back to the kitchen.

Rachael said, "Sadd's been telling me how she materialized at the airport, thrilled to think she was going to meet Herrick. Tell me, how do you like my wonderful grandson?"

Duck that one. I said, "First finish telling us about Annette — the suspense is killing me."

"Well" — Rachael put her almost untouched steak back on the counter — "it seems that a few summers ago Boyd was in some production at the Ogunquit Playhouse in Maine. Annette — she sews beautifully — was working on costumes, picking up extra cash. I guess she was rather hard up after her husband died. She said Boyd used to sit backstage and talk to her, and he finally admitted that she reminded him of *me*. Of course, Boyd has always known the family gossip about my father's wild oats, and while Annette is tiny and I'm a horse, genes do come out, as we

136

said, in traits like voice and features. Annette had no qualms about telling who she was — her mother had never deceived her — but she added that it was all ancient history and she had no desire to rattle any skeletons. But, Boyd, the eternal operator, saw it differently."

Rachael took pudding from the refrigerator and began to spoon it out.

"He suggested that she come here and offer her services to me as a companion — not telling me who she was, of course — and he would write to me about this worthy soul who was just the companion I needed. Actually, I'd been considering taking one on because I really shouldn't drive anymore. Boyd hinted to Annette that should I prove a sensitive soul who dreaded scandal, she could pick up some hush money and share it with him. She was horrified but said nothing because the prospect of a home and job in Dublin sounded so enticing. Of course we hit it off at once, and she told me the whole story the second day she was here."

Sadd said, "Did she buy it when he showed up as Armand?"

"Never. I told you I had some doubts at first, but Annette never did. Even though I described the extraordinary resemblance, Annette never bought it." Rachael put the spoon down slowly. "I don't know what I'd have done during those awful weeks that he was here if I hadn't had Annette to huddle with."

I said, eating pudding, "Why doesn't she live here with you?"

"Because she prefers not to. She's very independent. I found her a nice little flat in Sandymount, and that Mercedes" — Rachael smiled — "is the joy of her life."

Sadd began to laugh. "The Boyds of this world circle and circle and always end up — as we used to say in the air force — flying up their own ass."

"Right now," I said grimly, "the only place we know he's flying is Ireland. He'll be back eventually, you know that, don't you, Rachael?"

"Let him come," Rachael said defiantly. "I'll face him and tell him I've changed my will and left everything to Herrick and Annette."

"Good God, woman!" Sadd sputtered into his dish. "Do you want him to strangle you on the spot through sheer rage?"

"And have you made that change, dear?" I asked.

"No, but I plan to, just as soon as I can get down to Mr. Duffy's office."

"Rachael" — I stood up and started to clear the table — "Sadd's right, this man is capable of anything. He's got his plan rolling now, and anything that derails it could send him berserk. We're just going to have to play along with him till we can think of a way to trip him up or" — and I could hear the voice of Henry Gamadge — "make him trip *himself* up."

It was almost midnight when Rachael followed us to the front door. The cab pulled up as she opened it.

"You're not to stay in that hotel," she said. "I want you back here tomorrow — all three of you."

I said, "Now, Rachael —"

"Annette will pick you up first thing in the morning."

"Rachael," said Sadd, "there is simply no need —"

"Oh, dear, are you really only here for one week?"

Vee said, "Mrs. Shea, I don't feel that I should —"

"Well, then, we'll make the most of that week. Good night!"

We laughed as Rachael shut the door behind us.

In the misty midnight streets Dublin looked very romantic. The cabdriver asked us where we were from and said he had relatives in Newark, New Jersey. We said that was interesting because Newark wasn't far from New York, and by the time we'd exhausted that coincidence we were pulling up to the Gresham. There was a note in the box, which I took to be the one I'd left for Vee, but it was on greenish lined paper, addressed in a sprawling hand to "Vee of the Lovely Letters."

We all three looked at it and then at each other. Vee read it aloud as we walked to the elevator. " 'I shall pick you up tomorrow at eleven for a glorious, sun-glinting day in Phoenix Park. We shall have poetry and provender. I'll provide the poetry if you provide the provender.' "

At the last words we burst into such loud laughter that the desk clerk frowned at us across the quiet lobby. Smothering our merriment, we got into the elevator.

Sadd said, "Are you sure you can afford this sun-glinting admirer?"

"And are you to be picked up on that 'broken-down beast of a motorbike'?" I asked.

"That might be the only fun part," said Vee.

Sadd took out his key. "Just beware of passing any garages. You might be asked to sponsor some darlin' repairs."

"At least," said Vee, "I can shut my eyes and listen to him read his poetry."

I said, as we started down the hall to our

rooms, "Vee, I wouldn't say anything to Herrick about this Boyd-Armand business. Rachael hasn't discussed it with him." Sadd looked at me in surprise, and Vee said okay. "Here's the key. I'm going down to Mr. Saddlier's room to get a book. I can never get to sleep without reading first."

Vee let herself in, and we walked to Sadd's door. He said, "When did Rachael tell you that?"

"She didn't."

Sadd snapped on the light and said, "Nightcap?"

"Yes."

He poured from his flask of sherry, we sat down, and he said, "If Herrick's involved, we're letting Vee go joy-riding with a darlin' accomplice."

"How could we prevent her? I hope and pray he's *not* involved. Even so, I don't want her falling for him. There's something nutty about the guy, even . . . fishy."

"You mean besides being just a state-of-the-art bore?"

"Yes."

I got up and walked to the window, then back to my chair. I sat down again and said, "Sadd, Rachael's next."

"Don't say it." He sat motionless.

"I'll give Boyd a week to get here."

"And by that time we'll be gone." Sadd looked into his glass. "Maybe we'd better ring in Armand's daughter after all."

I shook my head. "We can't afford to endanger Vee."

"But Boyd doesn't know she's alive."

"Herrick does." I got up again and sat down again. "No, our only hope is Annette. She may know something or remember something or have something, possibly without realizing it. We'll just have to pump her."

13

I wasn't concerned till about ten o'clock.

The day was warm and bright, and breakfast at the Gresham had been excellent. We joked about what a great poet might like for "provender," and the waiter told Vee where she could get subs — he chuckled at the word — and beer nearby. She went off, leaving us over our third cup of coffee. When we transferred to the lobby, Sadd bought a paper and I went out to the street to watch for the Mercedes.

At ten-thirty I came back in, my hands turning to ice, and sat down next to Sadd. He said, not looking up from his paper, "Now, quit it. She's coming."

I said, "What day is today?"

He looked at the top of his paper. "Wednesday."

"What day did Armand die?" I was struggling with the sequence of events since lunch at the Dorrence.

Sadd lowered the paper and looked into space. "It seems like a lifetime ago, but actually it was only Monday."

People streamed by. The lobby buzzed.

I said, "He's got Annette, Sadd."

"Now, Clara —"

"She's the only one who never bought him for even one minute, and he must have sensed it. He couldn't chance it any longer."

"Dammit!" Sadd threw down the paper. "He can't have gotten here already unless he's a magician."

"He is." I was shaking. "I swear I think he *is* a magician. He only waited for Henry's call and then he got on a plane." It occurred to me dimly that Boyd had become "he," only "he." His name was anathema. "And even if he couldn't get here, maybe . . ." I looked down at my clenched hands. "Maybe there was Herrick."

Sadd said, "Now, listen to me, Clara: there could be ten reasons why Annette hasn't showed up. Maybe she — or Rachael — have been trying to get us on the phone while we're sitting down here fabricating horrors." He looked past me. "Here comes Vee. Don't say anything."

She came through the door with a big shopping bag and was headed for the elevator when she saw us.

"Hey!" She changed her course. "I thought you'd be gone by now. Hasn't Annette showed?"

"Not yet," I said. "I was just about to go upstairs and call Rachael."

"Want me to do it?"

"No, no. Isn't Herrick due shortly?"

"Not till eleven."

"I'll make the call." Sadd stood up. "I want to get a book anyway if we're spending the day there. By the way, are we taking Rachael up on her invitation and checking out of here?"

They looked at me expectantly, and I tried to sound casual. "No, I think we'd better stay put, for a day or two, at least."

As I spoke I realized I was looking at someone I'd seen before but couldn't instantly place. Then it came to me as the young man walked toward us.

"Isn't that Liam O'Coyle?"

Sadd and Vee turned, and he reached us and said, smiling, "I'm a very poor substitute, but Herrick just couldn't get away. Something completely unavoidable came up."

What is that expression? "My blood ran cold." I was only just aware that Liam was looking apologetic, Vee was looking mortified, and Sadd was looking at his watch. He said, moving away, "Nice to see you, Liam. I must make a phone call."

Vee started after him, clutching the provender. She said brightly, over her shoulder, "Tell him no problem. And I'm sure you're a busy guy. I wouldn't dream of —"

"Vee!" He said the name with urgency and sweetness. "Please don't be angry with him. And I was delighted when he asked me to come. I'll be quite honest: I was thrilled."

The rather nondescript young man who had accompanied his flamboyant friend was suddenly animated and charming. Through my shuddering dismay at the thought of what Herrick's "unavoidable" business might be, I was conscious that I wanted Vee to go. But I could only sit there. Liam took the bag from her arms, lifted out the sales slip, and put it in his pocket. He said, "We'll take care of that presently. Now, if you'll only come. Please, Vee."

It may have been the use of her name, or his vivid blue eyes, or his hand on her arm, but she smiled and shrugged and said, "Okay. Thanks."

Good kid, I thought. At least you're not going off with that other suspect character. Liam piloted her across the lobby, and she looked back at me and smiled. I waved, then sat more or less unable to move till the elevator door opened and Sadd came out, rather white-faced.

"There's no answer at Rachael's."

I knew there were cabs in waiting, and I just pointed to the front door. Neither of us said anything, and we got into the first one in line. I gave the driver Rachael's address in Herbert Park. He looked back at me in surprise.

"I picked up a lady at that house about an hour ago. You know her? Some friend of hers had an accident."

It took several seconds before I could speak, and Sadd appeared unable to. I said, "What happened?"

"Well, it seems" — he plunged into the traffic with an abandon that would have unnerved me an hour ago; now I was numb — "she got a call this morning from Sandymount, where a friend of hers has a flat. They told her the lady took a tumble down the stairs. She called a cab and got me and I drove her over. She asked me to wait. The police ambulance was there, but I guess there was nothing anybody could do."

"Her friend was dead," I said. It was a statement, not a question.

"Yes, it seems she broke her neck. My fare, the lady from Herbert Park, she was that stunned. I heard her ask where the body would

147

go, and they said St. Anthony's Hospital —
it's the nearest — and she said she'd take care
of everything but right now she was going
home. Officer Ryan — he's a nice lad — he
offered to drive her, but she said no, she had
me waiting."

"Was there anybody at her house when you
got there?" Sadd's voice was hoarse.

"Not that I saw. I helped her in the door,
and I said maybe I should tell a neighbor or
two she'd had a shock, but she said no, she had
some friends coming and she was sure they'd
be there soon. So I guess you're the —"

"Yes, we're the friends," I said. "Can you
hurry, really hurry?"

"Well, now, ma'am, I'll do my best, but
we don't want another accident, do we?"

Accident. No, we didn't want another accident. . . . The O'Connell Bridge, Baggot
Street, the American embassy, Trinity College
. . . the same route Annette had driven so
skillfully the night before — *that Mercedes
is the joy of her life.* " Now we were turning
into Herbert Park, its houses supremely elegant by daylight, and here was Rachael's.

Sadd had his wallet in hand, and I opened
the cab door and was out before it fully
stopped.

"Watch it, ma'am, you can break an ankle
that way." But I was already up the front walk.

I pushed open the front door and went straight into the living room. Rachael was huddled on the big chair, her eyes closed. She opened them dazedly as I went to her and knelt down and put my arms around her.

I said, "We heard it from the cabdriver. We just happened to get the same one." She gasped and shook. "And I want you out of this house."

"What?" She was blank. Sadd stood in the doorway, his hands in his hair.

I said, "Out. Right now. I wish we'd kept the cab."

"Clara, I can't —"

"Yes, you can. You can come straight back to the Gresham with us."

Sadd said, "If you don't mind — I have to sit down first."

I realized that I did, too. I pulled a straight chair next to Rachael, and Sadd went to a lacquer cabinet near the window.

"May I pour myself a brandy, Rachael?"

"Of course." It was a whisper. She was leaning back in her chair, eyes closed again. Another whisper. "He did it, didn't he?"

The sinister pronoun again. I said, "Yes — or somebody did it for him." I regretted the last words immediately, but they didn't seem to register with Rachael. I took her freezing hand between my own two freezing ones.

"Can you tell us what happened?"

"What happened? . . . Yes, what happened." This is important, she seemed to say, and I must get it right.

"When I woke up this morning I right away called Annette to tell her to pick up some bread at a bakery on Pembroke Street where they have the most wonderful —" Rachael gulped and looked lost, then focused again. "Well, there was no answer for the longest time. Annette doesn't have a phone, but her landlady, Mrs. Fermoyle, is nice about taking messages. Finally a man picked up and said he was Officer Ryan and there'd been an accident — one of the tenants had fallen downstairs. I asked who it was and he said he didn't know but here was Mrs. Fermoyle and then she came on and said, 'Oh, Mrs. Shea, it's your friend Annette, and she's broken her neck and I'm afraid she's dead.'" Rachael stopped, shakiness setting in again. "So I called a cab and went right over."

None of us spoke. I found myself casting dread looks at the long window, half expecting to see Boyd with his Peter Quint "white face of damnation" peering in. Then Rachael said, almost to herself, "How did he get here so soon?"

"Oh, he's a fast-moving gent," I said. "He doesn't have much time, and he knows it. But he's done for himself this time." I could feel my gorge beginning to rise and my voice to shake. "I don't care who this man is. He can be Armand, Boyd, or Boris Karloff. He's killed two people, and he's going to pay."

Sadd smiled into the fireplace. "Are you listening, Henry Gamadge?"

"Of course he's listening," Rachael said gently. "And so are Armand and Annette."

We both began to cry at this point, and Sadd said, "Pull yourselves together, girls. Rachael, you'd better pack some stuff."

She took my hand and struggled up from the chair. Neat, tailored Rachael in a disheveled skirt and blouse, her hair a mess. But she looked great in my eyes as she said, "Annette first. Come to the hospital with me. Then I must arrange for the funeral."

Sadd said, "Was she a member of your Friends?"

"No, Annette was a devout Catholic. She always went to the Pro Cathedral. That's where I'll have her mass. And I think . . . yes, Saint Martin's Cemetery. I'll have to decide . . ." Rachael's voice trailed as she seemed to realize she wasn't up for deciding much of anything.

I said, "We'll help. Then I want to go to her flat and ask some questions. Where's your car?"

"There."

Of course. My heart sank as Sadd said, "I'll get a cab and drive it back."

Rachael came to the rescue. "Sadd, dear, it's a trafficky trip, and if you're not used to driving here and you're not sure of the way . . ." Keep talking, Rachael. Then she blew it. "I'll call Herrick."

Sadd and I looked at each other in dismay, and I said quickly, "Does he — I mean — I seem to recall that he has no car."

"Of course he does. A very nice one. I gave it to him." Rachael looked at me in surprise as she dialed a number.

That liar. I walked to the bookcase and stood there, hoping she couldn't get the wretch on the phone. She couldn't. Mr. Shea would not be in till three o'clock, when he had a class.

"I'll dress and pack a bag," Rachael said, beginning to sound like herself. "Then we'll call a cab."

She started toward the door. I said, "Rachael, did Herrick meet, quote, Uncle Armand, when he was here?"

She stopped, her hand to her head. "I think . . . Yes, I invited Herrick to dinner once. I did it to reinforce Boyd's conviction that we were fooled. Of course I said nothing to Herrick about — about — because I didn't want him to be nervous or say something by mistake. It was bad enough for Annette and me." She was trembling and holding on to the doorjamb. Then she straightened. "I will *not* go to pieces." She reached the bottom step in the hall, then turned. "Oh, yes, Boyd went to one of Herrick's readings, I remember now. Herrick said they went to a pub afterward and had a chat."

She went up the stairs, her long frame suddenly, tragically bent. I could only lean against the bookcase and say to Sadd, "Thank God Vee isn't with him."

Sadd put down his brandy glass and said vehemently, "I don't believe it. I simply don't believe he's involved."

"Not even when he has a very nice car, given to him by his grandmother, which he doesn't bother to mention?"

"That hardly makes him an accessory to murder."

I went back to the straight chair and sat on the edge of it. I said, "Sadd, where is Boyd now?"

"Probably at some Dublin hotel practicing shock and dismay for when he hears about Annette."

I said, "Could he — or . . . or whoever it was — have been seen with Annette last night or early this morning or whenever? . . . I suppose we won't know till we go there and ask."

Sadd walked to the window. "What a lovely place this is. Who would think, walking in here, that we're drowning in horror."

I raised my eyes nervously to the ceiling. "I'm almost afraid to let her be up there alone. I have visions of Dracula scaling the wall."

Rachael's voice called reassuringly, "Clara, come help me decide what to take."

I leaped — if it can be called that — from my chair and hurried to the gracious, sloping staircase lined with family pictures. Rachael's mother was everywhere, as was her husband, as were Boyd and Armand, their identical faces smiling from group after group. Two steps from the top, I spotted myself and Rachael, arm in arm on the steps of the Trinita di Monte, in hats and white gloves. . . .

"Hats and gloves!" I exclaimed. "Hard to believe." Rachael looked out from the airy front bedroom. She said, "What?"

"That picture of us at the Trinita. When you think of the way kids dress now. I only remember that as a snapshot."

"Steven had it enlarged for me. It was always one of my favorites. I must take a shower. My suitcase is in that closet." Rachael took off her skirt and threw it on the bed. "Will you pull some underwear from the drawer? And Clara, I'm not going to be put out of my house indefinitely. I'll go to the hotel with you till after the funeral, then I'm coming back here." She was taking a robe from the back of the bathroom door. "And on Sunday I'm going to church, and at Centering Down I'll —"

"At what?"

"Centering Down. It's when we meditate and express our concerns aloud. I intend to put all this wickedness in the hands of God. Now, I feel better just having said that."

Rachael shut herself in the bathroom, and I heard the shower. I felt humble, even profane, in the face of such faith; but even then a practical apprehension came to me. Aloud? Did Rachael mean to denounce Boyd to the world? It seemed reckless. I hoped we were not in for a reenactment of *Murder in the Cathedral*.

I took out the suitcase — a dear old thing, more battered than my own — and put some underwear in it. Back to the closet for a couple of skirts and blouses — shoes? — Lord, it was difficult packing for someone else. From her dressing table I took face cream, hairspray — then stood transfixed.

In an old-fashioned silver frame embossed with cherubs was a photograph of the young man I knew as Liam O'Coyle. I picked it up and stared at the inscription till I knew I had it right: "For my dear Pix, appreciator and enabler, your loving grandson, Herrick."

The bathroom door opened and Rachael came out. "What is there about water? I feel so much —" She saw the photograph in my hand. "That doesn't do Herrick justice. Isn't he a dear?"

"Oh, he's a dear all right," I said, replacing the picture. "He calls you 'Pix'?"

"Yes." She laughed. "A silly name left over from his childhood when I read him stories about pixies."

"Have you ever met his friend, Liam O'Coyle?" I asked.

"Liam? Yes, he's been here a few times. Herrick says he's a fine editor. But I wish his wife would make him do something about his teeth. How's the packing?"

"Rachael, I'm going to let you finish. I better see how Sadd's doing. He's been pretty upset by all this."

"I'm sure he has, the poor dear. Do you remember how he and Boyd and Armand used to . . ."

She turned away and I went out of the room.

14

Sadd looked up from his book as I entered the living room.

I said, "I don't know what you're reading, but I bet I have a more interesting story."

"Oh?"

"There once was a young Irish poet named Herrick Shea whose grandmother kept a picture of him on her dressing table. He used to get fan letters from an adoring girl in New York, and when she wrote that she was coming to Dublin to meet him, he asked a friend named Liam O'Coyle to stand in for him in case the girl was — I believe the expression is — 'a dog.' Liam was to act like a jerk, and the girl would be disgusted and take off. When it turned out, however, that she was attractive and charming, our poet repented of the trick, came to take her on a picnic, and — one hopes — confess all."

Sadd had been gazing at me, first in bewilderment, then with a developing smile. Now he laughed.

"And there once was a suspicious woman from New York who was sure this poet was possibly a murderer, instead of just a careful guy who didn't want to get stuck with a 'dog.' I haven't heard that expression. Like all slang, it has a certain —"

"I almost hope Vee finds *him* a bore." I flounced to a chair. "Serve him right." I glared at Sadd's grin. "*You* are probably hoping they fall in love and all ends happily."

"Yes, I am rather."

Despite my sputtering I was feeling very relieved. "I suppose we can be grateful for Rachael's sake. I don't think she could have taken a third blow. . . ." And we were back in the nightmare again.

I got up and started walking around the room. "Sadd, Boyd is going to show up at this door after Annette is buried, commiserate with Rachael on both deaths, and offer to move in. He, her devoted brother, will not let her be alone. Situation made to order. First thing you know —"

"No." Sadd shook his head. "He couldn't risk a third death so soon."

"Where's the risk? Who would connect a drowning in New York with a fall downstairs in Dublin?"

"We would."

"But we'll be *gone*. Besides, we're locked

in to this appalling role of believers till we can find something to make him crack."

"Maybe" — Sadd closed his book and stood up — "we should ring in Armand's daughter after all, now that Vee is safe from Herrick, the Horrible Henchman."

"Too complicated," I said impatiently, "too far away, too long drawn out — I want something *now*. Annette's flat. We still haven't been there. Oh, God, if only somebody saw him." I began to pace again. "But I doubt it. He's such a — a —"

"Pro," said Sadd, and never had that simple little word sounded so chilling. "Perhaps he dropped an initialed handkerchief in the process of breaking Annette's neck. It seems the least he could do for us."

I went to the foot of the stairs and called, "Rachael, ready?"

"Just coming."

"Shall I call the cab?"

"Please. The number is on a list by the phone in the kitchen."

Sadd followed me down the hall. I said, over my shoulder, "I'm going to get two cabs, one to take me to Annette's place and the other to take you and Rachael to the hospital."

Sadd looked alarmed. "I think you should be with us. I'm not up to handling things if Rachael breaks down."

"She won't break down." I was running my finger down the list. "You heard what she said just now — 'I will *not* go to pieces.' "

"She said that standing here in her own house, not hovering over a dead friend."

"Sadd, there will be no hovering." I was dialing. "Identification isn't necessary."

"She'll want to look at her friend. And so would I. And so would you."

He said it so simply, and it rang so true, that I had no reply. The cab line was busy. Rachael came down the back stairs into the kitchen, looking more like her old self in a good-looking black wool suit.

I said, "Sadd will go to the hospital with you, dear. I want to get to Annette's flat. I might find something or hear something we can use."

She nodded. "I'll go there myself in a few days and get her things. For now, will you bring something for — for her to wear?"

I gulped. The thought of pawing through the poor thing's clothes . . . Sadd planted himself squarely between us.

"Now, look here — we should *not* separate. I, for one, am scared to death of meeting Boyd coming toward me down a hall or up a street or around a corner. Let's stick together. All go to the hospital, then all go to the flat."

Rachael said, locking the kitchen door, "I think I agree."

I dialed again, got the promise of a cab in ten minutes, and we walked to the front door. Sadd opened it, and we saw Boyd coming up the walk, his cab pulling away.

The Gorgon's head. That was the image that flashed through my mind as we stood turned to stone. I think even the shield of Hercules could not have saved us from petrification. The memory of my son's words of warning to himself enabled me to gasp, "Remember to call him *Armand!*"

He stretched out his arms at sight of us. "You dear, dear people! I came as quickly as I could to be with you. We must just keep saying, 'He's at rest, our poor Boydie is at rest.' "

By this time he was on the step, embracing Rachael. I was next to get the viper's kiss, then he grasped Sadd's limp hand. He did not, of course, appear to notice that he was in the company of three mutes, but went on briskly, "You're going someplace. May I tag along? Give me two minutes for the bathroom and I'll be with you."

Thank God for the call of nature, which gave us those two minutes to recover ourselves somewhat. I made sure the heavy front door was closed behind him, and Sadd said quickly,

"We mustn't appear to huddle. I'll stand out there and watch for the cab. Do we take him with us?"

"Oh, no," Rachael said weakly.

"Oh, yes," I said firmly. "We're going to rub his nose in it."

"My God, he must have a very strong stomach to show up now." Sadd shook his head and went down the path. Rachael, very white, was holding on to the iron railing of the three steps.

"Darling, let me do the talking," I said, my arm around her.

"Oh, please. And just don't let him sit next to me."

The door opened and Boyd came out. He said at once, "There's something wrong — I know it. Please tell me."

Sure, Boyd — ready if you are. I said, "There's been a second tragedy, Armand. Annette's dead."

His Academy Award performance was something to see. He stared at me, then steadied himself against the house. I think he even managed to turn a little pale. Well he might. It was the first time he'd heard the deed put into words. He said chokingly, "How? When?"

I said, "We can talk in the cab." Sadd was flagging it to the curb. Rachael, still clinging to the railing, started down the steps, and Boyd sprang to her side. I said, "Rachael, let me have your key." She got it from her pocketbook, I locked the front door and followed. Boyd looked back at me.

"Where are we going? And you still haven't told me how —"

"To the hospital, then to make arrangements for the funeral," I said.

Sadd put Rachael into the backseat and got in after her with the words, "Can we put you in front, Armand?"

"Of course."

But I kept him on the street, looked into his eyes, and said, "Annette fell down the stairs to her flat and broke her neck. Last night or this morning." He gasped. "We're going to the hospital now. After that to her flat to get some things. It would help if you came with us."

His eyes never left my face. "Of course. Anything. Anything at all. But must it be now? I just got in, and of course I'm incredibly shocked. Perhaps instead of going with you now, if I just go inside and wait till . . ."

Oh, no, Boydie. You're not going back in that house to put your feet up and plan the next move. Sadd put his head out. "Are we off?"

"Right away," I said. "We must go to

Annette's flat today, Armand. Rachael's car is there. Can you drive it back?"

"That Mercedes? Good God, no. The driving in Dublin is mind-boggling. Annette was a wonder — she mastered it in no time. But don't put me behind that wheel if you value your life."

I'd have preferred a condition slightly less close to the bone. Boyd got in the front seat and I in the back, and Rachael said, "Saint Anthony's Hospital."

It was a ghastly ride. Boyd became chatty and solicitous.

"How simply awful for all of you. I became very fond of Annette in just the short time I knew her. Rachael" — he turned and patted her hand, and she jerked violently — "did you tell them that Boyd found Annette for you? I suppose we can thank him for that."

"Yes, she told us," said Sadd.

Boyd went on, half turned toward us. "I've had his ashes sent to Grosse Pointe. I was going to bury them in the garden there, but since I'm selling the house I thought I'd take them out to a little community theater on Route Three that Boydie loved and sprinkle them near there. Do I sound hopelessly sentimental?"

The utter gall of the man. Rachael was straining not to look at him, and I kept my eyes on the streets of the city that I longed to enjoy.

"And Rachael, dear" — another pat from Boyd, another jerk from Rachael — "I want you to know that I'm here for just as long as you need me. I'm at the Jury, but if you'd like me —"

"Clara and Sadd are with me now," Rachael said quickly. "Thank you . . ." She got it out: "Armand."

"How long will you be here?" He glanced from me to Sadd.

"The rest of the week," I said with reluctance.

"But we're thinking of taking Rachael back to New York with us," Sadd announced airily.

Boyd frowned. "I'm not sure that would be wise. A double tragedy like this can do a job on the morale. Not that my sister isn't a very strong lady" — pat, jerk — "but I don't want you to go into a depression and find yourself far from home, darling. I honestly think you should be in your own house."

Naturally. Her own house is the very best place for an elderly woman to be when she is depressed and brooding and perhaps thinking about ending her life. . . .

The driver said, "Here's Saint Anthony's. What entrance?"

"The emergency, I expect," said Sadd. We

circled the big old building, and the cab came to a stop.

Rachael said quietly, "I'd rather go in alone. I know you'll understand. I'll try not to be long."

I got out so she could, kissed her, and said, "Let me come." She shook her head, took some bills from her purse, thrust them at the driver, and walked into the hospital.

The cab went off, and the three of us stood on the cement sidewalk of the jammed parking lot, looking everywhere but at each other. Sadd said, "I presume there's a waiting room."

We walked through the automatic doors and into a hall lined with chairs. A dozen anxious-faced persons sat there; one woman was crying. I wasn't sure I could take this for too long. I said, "I'd love a cup of coffee. There must be a cafeteria."

"In the next building." A nurse smiled as she passed us.

Boyd said virtuously, "But Rachael will look for us here. You two go. I'll wait."

You sanctimonious bastard, I thought in sudden rage, and sat down determinedly. "You two go. I'll wait."

Sadd said, "Is that my cue to say, 'You two go, I'll wait'? We sound like the Three Stooges."

"The fox, the goose, and the bag of grain,"

I said, and began to giggle a little hysterically. Heads turned, and I was ashamed and buried my nose in my pocketbook, looking for a tissue. Sadd and Boyd sat down on either side of me. "Surely you remember the fox, the goose, and the bag of grain?"

They looked at me blankly, and I babbled on. "Henry Gamadge used to say —"

"And bless his memory!" Boyd said devoutly. I wanted to bat him.

"He used to say that sometimes in the midst of tragedy one can be reminded of something comical. 'You two go, I'll wait' reminded me of the fox, the goose, and the bag of grain. Neither of you have heard the puzzle?"

"Neither of you *has* heard the puzzle," said Sadd. " 'Neither' is a singular subject."

"I certainly haven't," said Boyd. "Have you, Sadd?"

"Not only have I not heard it" — Sadd's face told me I was being a bore — "but I'm in a perfect frenzy of desire *never* to hear it."

"Just for that I'll tell it." Anything was better than just sitting there, but it wasn't till I got toward the end that I recognized the subtle possibility inherent in this little puzzle that had delighted me as a child. I folded my hands and kept my voice low.

"There was once a farmer who was taking three things to market: a fox, a goose, and a bag of grain. He came to a river and was able to get a small rowboat, but then he realized he had a problem. The boat was only big enough to take him and *one* of his three items. But if he took the fox across first, the goose would eat the grain, and if he took the grain across, the fox would eat the goose. The only two that could be safely left together were the fox and the grain. At some point, the fox and the goose, or the goose and the grain, would have to be left together. How did he get them all across?"

Sadd said at once, suppressing a yawn, "I give up," but Boyd was the dogged good scout. He wrinkled his brow and said:

"Now, that is a poser. . . . He takes the grain . . . No, that won't work. . . ."

A car came to a sudden stop outside the door, and a woman hurried in with a bawling child clutching a puffy wrist. The years rolled back, and I was plucking Paula from beneath a swing. . . .

I said, feeling suddenly tired, "The farmer takes the goose across first. He leaves her on the bank and goes back and gets the fox. He takes the fox across, puts it on the bank, and takes the goose back with him. He leaves her there, takes the bag of grain over, puts it with the fox, and rows back to get the goose."

Boyd slapped his knee. Sadd stood up and said, "I'll be the goose and leave you two here while I go get coffee."

I laughed. "I'll be the bag of grain — I have the figure for it. so Armand" — I smiled at him — "we'll call you the Fox."

I put it in upper case for all I was worth, and for an instant I thought I saw panic in his face. Then he looked past me and said:

"Here's Rachael."

15

At sight of Rachael's drawn face I suddenly felt almost unclean in the company of this man. I said, "Armand, will you call us a cab? The phone is just outside — I can see it from here."

He hastened out, and Sadd and I closed in on Rachael. She said with her eyes closed, "Get rid of him. I don't care where he goes or what he does or how he tries to kill me — just get rid of him!"

How he tries to kill me. No illusions.

Sadd said, "One more minute and I'll throttle him. Why must we be saddled with him? What do you have in mind, Clara?"

I had nothing in mind, which was upsetting in the extreme. My notion of taking Boyd with me to Annette's flat suddenly seemed absurd. Surely Boyd, the fox, had made certain he was the invisible fox. I wrenched my mind back to Rachael.

"We'll send him back to the Jury. He says he's booked there, so he has to be. Your house is locked, that's a consolation. We wouldn't want to find him waiting for us there."

Through the glass door I was watching Boyd circling impatiently around the man who was using the phone. Off guard, his face was haggard and tense. Rachael had turned her back to the door, but Sadd was watching him, too. He said, "The guy's an exhausted wreck. He's my age, he has heart trouble, and he's been on stage almost continuously for weeks. I'd be flat out at this point — with or without a bad conscience."

I said, "He probably desperately needs to rest. Play along with what I say."

A cab pulled up to the door and disgorged a teenage boy with a gash in his head and a woman holding a bloodied towel. As they stumbled past us I saw Boyd signal to the cabdriver. Then he hurried in.

"Got one."

"Armand," I said as Rachael turned away and bent over the water cooler, "this is where we part company for a while."

"Oh?" His relief was instant.

"We feel you should go back to your hotel and rest. You've been under a terrific strain. And Rachael, exhausted as she is, refuses to put off a dinner party tonight for Herrick and his fiancée's family."

A spurt of water shot up into Rachael's face,

and Sadd, his mouth twitching, gave her his handkerchief.

"Herrick's engaged?" Boyd was polite. "How nice. He didn't tell me when I was here."

"It's very recent." I was propelling him toward the door. "And of course, Rachael shouldn't even try —"

"But, being Rachael, of course she *will* try. What a saint. Actually, I can use some rest." We were outside now, and Boyd opened the cab door. "Give me a day or two and I'll be more like myself."

Be more like yourself, Boyd, and the heavens will cry for vengeance. I said, "Naturally you'll come to the funeral."

"Oh, absolutely. Let me know when."

"And the wake."

"Wake?" He half turned. "Is that still done?"

"It is in Ireland, I'm sure. Anyway, I'll be in touch."

The cab drove off as a small white Toyota buzzed into the parking lot. I thought, One more gash, break, sprain, or concussion and *I'll* be a candidate for here. I went back into the hall and said to Sadd, "Wasn't the goose going for coffee?"

He grinned and went. Rachael said, "What does that mean?" and sat down. I sat beside her.

"It means we are blessedly free of Boyd for a while and can take you home and put you down for a good rest. We'll get a cab — my God, we're subsidizing the cab companies of Dublin — but who can drive your car?"

"Herrick."

Herrick. Had he leveled with Vee yet? Rachael went on wistfully, "I wish what you said about his having a fiancée was true. I did like that girl so much. Don't laugh, but if Vee were to —"

"I'm not laughing. Did you know they're on a picnic together right now?"

Rachael looked at me in pleased surprise, and I said, "Rachael, what do you have planned for Annette?"

She straightened. "A wake at Brady's tomorrow. I just called them. Only for a couple hours. She — she knew so few people. . . . An open coffin. That's usual here, and her neighbors will expect it. Besides" — she looked at me grimly — "I want Boyd to look at her."

"So do I."

"Suppose he doesn't come?"

"He'd have to have one heck of a good excuse."

Sadd came through the door, clutching three cups of coffee between his hands. I relieved him of two as the white Toyota I'd seen entering the parking lot slid to a stop before the door and Vee jumped out. She came straight in and put her arms around Rachael.

"Oh. Mrs. Shea, I'm so sorry! We heard about Annette."

"How?" I asked, rescuing Rachael's coffee.

"Herrick tried to call you" — Oh, he was Herrick, was he? — "and when you didn't answer he tried Annette's and they told him. They said you'd probably be here. What can we do? Herrick is trying to park — Oh, I'm so awfully sorry!"

Despite Vee's genuine concern and sympathy, there was a light in her eye and a lilt in her pronunciation of "Herrick" that betokened imminent love, love, love. Of course she only knew half the tragedy, so it would once more be our delightful job to . . . Rachael kissed her and thanked her as Herrick came through the door. His face was as red as his hair — as well it might be, I thought sternly — and this time Sadd grabbed the endangered coffee as Herrick embraced his grandmother.

"It's awful, Pix, simply awful. Thank God these wonderful folks are here with you." He looked sheepishly from me to Sadd. "I feel like a fool."

"Why, dear?" asked Rachael.

I said, "Herrick, we need to get out of here."

"Of course you do. Where's the Merce? I'll take you home in that, and Vee can follow in my car. Okay, Vee?"

She nodded, lost in his eyes, and I felt a rush of impatience, especially as Sadd was gazing at them fatuously. I explained that the "Merce" was still at Annette's and that none of us dared drive it for fear of another casualty.

"Ah, to be sure — very wise. Then we shall all have to pack into my shrimp."

We did, and I thought of our ride from the airport only the day before and the silent young man at the wheel who now spoke with such warmth and authority.

"Can you bear to tell me about it, Pix?"

"When we get home, dear. I hope you can stay a bit."

"An hour or two. I have a class at three-thirty. But I can give you the whole weekend. What arrangements have you made?"

"Only for the wake at Brady's. I'd like to have Annette buried from the Pro Cathedral."

"Would you? A curate there, Father Ben Gargan, is in one of my classes. Shall I ask him to take care of it for you?"

"Oh, would you, dear? I'd be very grateful." Rachael leaned back and closed her eyes. "I'm afraid I'm quite paralyzed by the other horrible aspect of the thing."

Herrick braked sharply, and Rachael

opened her eyes, realizing what she'd said. Vee turned with a startled look, and Rachael said, "I'm sorry — I didn't mean to — as soon as we get home I'll —"

"Right now," said Herrick.

He turned into the parking lot of a small mall and stopped the car. "Talk, Pix. What horrible aspect?"

Rachael gulped and looked at me, and I looked at Sadd. He said, "Annette's death was not an accident."

Vee's reaction was immediate and appalling. She went as white as paper, put her hands to her head, and broke into sobs that were half screams. Herrick, nearly as white, looked at her in horror and dismay. Rachael moaned, "Why did I say anything, *why?* . . ."

Sadd got out of the car and opened the door next to Vee. She shook her head and pulled it shut again.

"I'm okay. Okay. Okay. See? I've stopped. Thank you, Mr. Saddlier, but I'm okay. Just keep going, Herrick, *please.*" Terrible gulps.

Herrick said, "What in God's name is it? What's it about? Will somebody please tell me?"

"I'll never forgive myself." Rachael put both her hands on Vee's shoulders and buried her face in her arms.

Sadd got back in the car and said, "Better

go ahead, Herrick."

"Not till I hear exactly what happened."

I said, "We believe Annette was murdered, and this is the second shock of its kind for Vee in two days. The story goes back a way, Herrick. If you'll just get us home, we'll explain in full."

He took Vee's hand, her fingers closed on his convulsively, and she nodded.

No one spoke till we turned into Rachael's driveway. Herrick drove down it to the rear of the house, stopped the car, and got out. He hotfooted it around to Vee's door and drew her out. He said, "You're coming in with me right now and get a brandy."

Vee allowed herself to be led to the back door steps. Rachael leaned forward and called, "It's locked. Here's the key to the front —"

But they disappeared inside.

We sat staring at the half-open kitchen door. Rachael said, trancelike, "I locked that."

"And I locked the front," I said, equally trancelike.

Sadd said, making it three, "And I watched you both."

He got out of the car and stood leaning on it, looking at the house. I followed, then Rachael. We stood in silence till I said, using the awful pronoun, "He'd never break and enter."

Sadd moved. "Let's look." I took Rachael's arm and, more or less supporting each other, we followed Sadd up the steps. He examined the lock and said, "No damage."

Inside we heard Herrick's and Vee's voices. I said, "Not a word to them — agreed?"

They nodded, and we stood staring at the intact lock. It was the kind you can set and it locks after you.

"Then how did he get in?" Rachael seemed so sated with horrors that she'd become matter-of-fact.

Sadd said, "Cellar? Ground-floor window?"

She shook her head. "I'm reasonably safety conscious, but Annette was a — a —"

"A security nut?" I asked, my mind burrowing toward the light.

"Absolutely. She went around before she left every night and —" Rachael could manage no more.

I said, "Do these words sound familiar? I quote: 'Give me two minutes in the bathroom.' "

I felt their impact as I spoke them. Sadd cleared his throat and nodded. "A simple matter to reset this and have the unlocked door waiting for him."

We stood there assimilating this, then Rachael said slowly, "But surely . . . he'd set it again as he left. Do you suppose . . . he's still in there?"

The thought was so frightful that now we were truly mute. I forced my mind into a quick calculation.

"I told him we were going from the hospital to Annette's flat. He assumes we're still dependent on cabs. He couldn't know that Herrick would arrive and whisk us straight home. What would be the hurry? I don't think he's been here yet."

16

We walked into the kitchen, and Herrick and Vee came to meet us. Her color was better. Herrick pulled chairs from the kitchen table and said, "Please, everybody sit. Vee's been filling me in, but she wants you to go over it in case she's missed anything."

I said, "Herrick, your grandmother needs a cup of tea or some of that brandy, and I need the bathroom."

Good God, I sounded like Boyd; but my need was genuine. I asked Sadd to give the account — he'd be more succinct than I — and I went upstairs to Rachael's bathroom. I am not, as I have said, prescient, but I truly believe I'd have known it if Boyd Evers was in that house. I looked quickly in all the bedrooms and all the closets and was on my way to the attic stairs when, passing the hall window, I saw his cab.

It was coming down the beautiful broad street very slowly. As it came abreast of

Rachael's driveway it almost stopped, then picked up speed and was gone. The shadowy figure in the back had undoubtedly seen Herrick's car.

Was Boyd now wondering — in a panic, I hoped — if we'd discovered the unlocked kitchen door? Perhaps we hadn't noticed or remembered having locked it. . . . In all the sorrow and confusion, it would be difficult to be sure . . . and probably we'd forgotten his request for those two minutes in the bathroom. He'd sweat till he got back to the hotel. Then I'd better call him and be chatty about the wake. That would be the all clear. Mustn't let him be too worried for too long and act precipitously.

I went down to the kitchen to find four silent people drinking tea. Herrick pulled out a chair, filled a cup for me, and said, "Let me be absolutely certain of all this. You have no actual proof that this man is *not* Armand Evers?"

"No."

"And no concrete evidence that he did either killing — if they were killings?"

"No."

My "no" twice was pretty sobering, even to me. Herrick looked at Vee, then into his mug. Rachael said, "Herrick, there are other things besides what you call 'concrete evidence.' If we —"

"Pix, dear" — he put his hand on hers — "I don't doubt your judgment, or Mr. Saddlier's, or Mrs. Gamadge's" — he looked around at us with earnest blue eyes — "and people get away with murder every day. But if this man is impersonating someone else, he simply cannot get away with it for long. Not in today's world. I mean, he's bound to be caught."

"We agree with you, Herrick," said Sadd. "He'll certainly be caught. We'd just prefer that he not kill your grandmother first."

All eyes turned to Rachael, who was sipping her tea and holding Vee's hand. Herrick said, "Pix, maybe you'd better lam out of here for a while."

"Go back to New York with us?" I said.

Vee nodded vigorously, and Sadd said, "Hear! Hear!" but Rachael, apparently revived by her tea, smiled almost serenely.

"No need," she said. "Clara has three more days. That's plenty of time for a Gamadge to work it out."

The respectful silence smote at my spirits. I said, trying to sound confident, "We still haven't been to Annette's flat. Who's up for it now?"

Herrick and Vee were on their feet. I added quickly, "Not you, Rachael. You're to stay here and rest, and Sadd stays with you."

"Thank you," said Sadd. "My knees don't love the backseat of that car."

"And we can bring the Merce back," said Herrick.

"We're going to eat something first." Rachael got up and went to the refrigerator.

Vee said, "And I'm going to fix it for you guys — we've had our picnic." She gently propelled Rachael out of the kitchen. Sadd followed, announcing that he was going to build himself a fire and read. Herrick and I, left alone, looked at each other. Then he came and put his hands on my shoulders.

"What must you think of me?" he said.

"It doesn't matter what I think. What does Vee think?" As if I didn't know.

"She's been super. And once we got laughing about it, it didn't seem to matter that I'd been a jackass." He walked away, then turned and looked at me again. "This is not an excuse or an alibi, but something happened a month or so ago that made me very leery of female fans. I'd been getting letters from a woman in Belfast, telling me that I was the world's greatest poet, etc., etc., and that one of these days she was going to travel down and tell me so to my face. Well, she did that. The only problem was that she arrived bag and baggage, announcing that she was going to stay and take care of me and that her husband and three children would have to be sacrificed on the altar of poetry."

We laughed, and I thought of Sadd's words, "Poets are catnip to women."

Herrick went on, "When I proposed that silly switch, Liam jumped at the idea of playing me. He's a frustrated actor, I do believe" — his voice changed — "and speaking of acting, Mrs. Gamadge, I find this matter of Boyd Evers incredibly bizarre. When he was last here he came to a reading of mine at Trinity. We had a drink afterward, and he was charm itself."

"What did you talk about?"

"Family, mostly. He was full of all sorts of stories about his boyhood and his sister Rachael and his cousin Boyd, the indigent actor, and how much they looked alike."

I went to the phone and took the directory from a shelf. I said, "Herrick, will you see if you can help Mr. Saddlier? He may be setting the house on fire."

He laughed and went. I found the number of the Jury and rang it. Boyd picked up almost immediately.

He was delighted to hear from me. Had we gone to Annette's? No? We'd decided to get Rachael straight home? Very wise. The wake was tomorrow? He'd be there. The funeral was Friday? He'd be there. Were we still thinking of taking Rachael back to New York with us? He'd advise against it, but that was up to Rachael. We should try to convince her that he'd be only too happy to move straight in with her. And thank you for calling, Clara, dear.

My voice had been warm and reassuring, with no echoes of unlocked doors. I hung up wondering for the first time what Boyd had expected to find, or do, once he had admitted himself. A quick search for Rachael's will, perhaps?

I took some apples from the refrigerator and a box of graham crackers from a shelf, put them on a tray, and walked into the living room, where a fire blazed merrily. Sadd looked at the tray and said, "Another one of your gourmet lunches?"

Vee came down the stairs to announce that Rachael was already half-asleep and wanted nothing to eat. I picked up one of the apples and said, "Let's go."

The drive to the Sandymount area of Dublin took us through streets I hadn't seen before. I asked Herrick to talk about Dublin and not to stop till we reached Annette's flat; it was probably the one opportunity I'd have to learn anything unconnected with death and disaster about this marvelous city. He did talk, and charmingly, but even so I was wretchedly distracted. I looked at Vee's profile turned adoringly toward him and vowed I'd not let this nightmare touch her more closely. Now Herrick was talking about fairy rings, circles of stones marking graves from Celtic times that still existed all over Ireland — there was one behind a house in Herbert Park — and that were sacred even from developers. One of his poems, he said, was called "The Barrow Grave," and Vee promptly recited it.

I had just so many hours left. . . .

Annette's street was pleasant if not elegant, with rows of houses, most of them, Herrick said, divided into flats. Some had garages. Annette's house did not, and the Mercedes was housed a few doors down. Here we were.

A round-faced, middle-aged woman in a bright yellow housedress and brown sweater opened the door and called to Herrick that she'd been worried about the car and had gone down to be sure the garage door was locked.

"Thank you, Mrs. Fermoyle." He got out, and we followed. She came a few steps down the walk and said How was poor Mrs. Shea? Herrick introduced us, and she shook hands.

"Come in, come in."

Oh, Boyd, you lucky monster, what a setup!

Directly to the left and inside the front door was another door. An enclosed stairway led

186

straight up from it. We climbed up, and Mrs. Fermoyle unlocked the door at the top. She switched on a light. The tiny flat was rather dark, perhaps because the curtains were drawn. Mrs. Fermoyle opened them, revealing the neatest little parlor I'd ever seen. Not a dish, not a magazine, not a sweater, not a tea towel, lay about. Was Annette a pathological neatnik, or had someone moved about, examining, checking, tidying up?

Mrs. Fermoyle said sympathetically, "This isn't easy for you, Mrs. Gamadge. How well did you know Mrs. Pine?"

Mrs. Pine? Of course — Annette Pine. "We only met her last night when we arrived," I said, including Vee with a gesture.

Mrs. Fermoyle said, "She thought the world of this one." She looked at Herrick. "She said he taught her to drive and praised her a lot, and said she was as good as any Dubliner. Take a chair, won't you."

I felt sick and sad. Herrick and Vee just stood there. Mrs. Fermoyle sat disconsolately on the sofa and looked at me. "You're from the States, aren't you? I remember she said last night that Mrs. Shea had company from the States. Mrs. Pine was from there herself, but French way back. When she came in last night it was the last time I saw her."

I said, trying not to sound investigative,

"Did she have a dizzy spell, do you think?"

"That, or she could have dropped a parcel or something and tripped over it. The mat's smooth" — slightly defensive — "you can see it is, so it couldn't have been that."

We all gazed at the mat and agreed it was as smooth as could be.

I said, edging as close as I dared, "Maybe she was excited about having company — maybe somebody came to see her."

"Mrs. Pine never had a soul come see her except Mrs. Shea. 'Least, nobody I ever saw. But then this flat has a private entrance with its own bell, so yes, maybe."

Yes, maybe. I stood up, wanting to ask if anyone else might have seen a visitor, but I could hardly canvas the neighborhood. I said, "Mrs. Shea will come later to get her belongings. Right now I'll pick out something from her closet. . . ."

This was Mrs. Fermoyle's meat. "She was such a tiny thing, but she always looked smart. There's a nice two-piece blue knit."

I followed her into the bedroom. Again, neat, neat, neat. Mrs. Fermoyle opened the closet and took out the knit on its hanger.

"Whereabouts is she?"

I racked my brains. "I think Mrs. Shea said — er — Brady's?"

Mrs. Fermoyle nodded. "On Island Street.

I could take it over there if you like, and anything else they want."

"That would be a very big favor, Mrs. Fermoyle. By the way, where is Annette's pocketbook?"

"I have it downstairs. I came and got it first thing. There's no trusting anybody at a time like this."

I was liking Mrs. Fermoyle more and more. I said, "Is there a desk?"

"In the kitchen. I had a little place fixed up there for a tenant to use."

We went back through the living room, where Herrick and Vee stood looking out the window. I smiled at them and followed Mrs. Fermoyle into the kitchen. Here, at least, were signs of living — a tea cup in the sink, some groceries on the counter. On a shelf in one corner with a chair before it were a pair of glasses and a note-pad and pencil. No letters. I was looking for a bank book, possibly in her pocketbook. The wastebasket, as far as I could see, contained only magazines and catalogs. I hesitated to rummage.

"She didn't do a lot of cooking," said Mrs. Fermoyle. "She said she mostly ate at Mrs. Shea's."

I nodded, realizing the place would yield nothing, and we went back to the living room. Vee was holding a worn leather picture frame.

She said, "This was on the windowsill."

"It's her and her mother," said Mrs. Fermoyle. "She told me once. I don't know who the other lady with the baby is."

I did.

"My mother was a rather remarkable woman for her time. She went to see the girl. . . . Can you picture the scene? . . . little Rachael and little Annette looking at each other from their mothers' laps."

I looked at the two women in the picture. Grosse Pointe plain, French fancy. I said, "May I take this with me for Mrs. Shea?"

"You certainly may." Mrs. Fermoyle gave the picture a swipe with her sleeve, and we went down stairs. "I'll just get that pocketbook for you." She disappeared into her own place, and we went out to the street.

"Vee," I said, "are you sure you can handle the drive back?"

She looked surprised, even a little indignant, so I shut up. Herrick said, with a rather unfortunate choice of words, "I'll give her a crash course in driving on the left. A quick spin should do it. Be right back, Mrs. Gamadge." He took Vee's hand and they got into his car.

Mrs. Fermoyle came out of the house with the pocketbook and I took it and I walked down the street to the garage she had pointed out. I unlocked the door with a key on

Annette's ring, and climbed into the front passenger seat of the Mercedes. I opened the big, square black pocketbook and took everything out. There, sure enough, was her bank book. No huge amount, though most of it undoubtedly representing Rachael's generosity. A check marked "August salary" was tucked in, ready for deposit.

I put everything back in, zipped the pocketbook, and heaved it onto the backseat. I slid the ignition key into place, then sat waiting for Herrick, overcome with anger.

A walk down a quiet street after dark. A ring of the bell. A climb up the stairs. A fatal blow to the neck. A climb down the stairs to deposit Annette's little crumpled frame. A walk back down the quiet, dark street.

I was suddenly weeping tears of frustration. I fumbled in my own pocketbook for a tissue — nothing — maybe there was a box in the glove compartment. I opened it.

A long white envelope lay there, addressed in a small, neat hand to — Where were my glasses? I found them, dropped them, cursed them, trod on them, picked them up, and finally got them on my face. Addressed to a law firm in Portland, Maine. The envelope was fat and sealed but unstamped, probably on its way to the post office to be weighed.

I opened it without a single pang of conscience. Annette's will with a note attached in the same small hand.

The will, a quick look showed me, was a simple matter leaving everything to Rachael. It was the note — I had to scan it fast, as Herrick was approaching — filled with mention of love and God — that gave me an ungodly idea.

17

We checked out of the Gresham late that afternoon. Sadd, told not to budge from Rachael's side, instructed me in the strict accounting of his books; I would probably find one or two in the bathroom and possibly a couple under the bed. Herrick picked us up after his class, and we arrived at Herbert Park to find Sadd mixing drinks and Rachael at the top of the stairs.

"Come on up," she called. "Clara, I've put you and Vee in the back guest room. It has a nice view of the garden. Sadd's on the third floor in Steven's study. There's a chair lift. I had it put in when Steven couldn't manage the stairs anymore."

We went up and found charming quarters, Sadd rode aloft and rode down again to say what a splendid room and did Rachael mind if he never left. She laughed and said not at all, and we went back downstairs.

Herrick was draining a glass of beer. He

said, "I thought I might take Vee over to Trinity. A friend of mine has an exhibit of watercolors. And we'll get a bite."

I watched them go, thinking, "Hello, young lovers . . ." and all that. Indeed, indeed, I'd had a love of my own and knew how it felt to have wings on my heels — but enough, Clara, back to business.

We sat down, and Sadd handed Rachael and me martinis. She said, "This was Steven's favorite drink. An American friend showed him how to make them."

I said, "Rachael, look at this." I put the envelope containing Annette's will in her lap but kept the note. She put her glass down and opened the envelope slowly. I looked at Sadd and said, "Annette's will."

He got up and went behind Rachael's chair and looked over her shoulder. They read in silence for a minute, then Sadd said, "Simplicity. An excellent thing in a woman."

"I thought that was a soft, low voice," I said.

"Can't there be more than one excellent thing in a woman?" Sadd went back to his chair. "Will you be a very much richer lady, Rachael?"

"No." Rachael was smiling a little sadly. "She had a couple of bonds that are in my safe deposit box, and a savings account, I think, but nothing else. Was this in her flat, Clara?"

"No, in the glove compartment of your car. On its way to the post office, I believe."

"Post office?" Rachael was staring at the will abstractedly. "You know, she and I talked about changing this just a few weeks ago. Oh, dear. I wish she'd had a chance to do it."

"She did." I held up the note. "This was attached." Rachael reached for it eagerly. "All we need is a fresh envelope and some stamps and presto — change."

"Oh, *good!*" She was beaming.

Sadd said, "Will somebody please explain?"

Rachael picked up her drink and leaned back in her chair. "Annette was such a little saint. She gave money to everybody from Mother Teresa to the Girl Scouts. And she loved doing it."

"The quintessential soft touch," said Sadd.

"Not really. She was just generous. I think she'd been that way all her life, which is one reason she never had much money. She had a favorite charity — some mission in Africa" — Rachael glanced at the note — "and she'd get letters from them thanking her and sending her pictures of the children, and she'd show them to me and say wasn't it wonderful she could do this —"

"And wasn't it wonderful," I said, "that

195

now she had you to help her do it."

"Well, that's what brought up the subject of the change." Rachael sat forward, her face animated. "Annette made a will when she came to Ireland. She'd never had one, and I insisted she do it. She told me she'd left everything to me and I could give it to charity if I liked. Well, one day we got talking about which of us would 'go first' and what we wanted the other one to do and so forth, and I said, 'Annette, why don't you change your will and leave everything directly to your mission, that's much more sensible.' Now, I'm glad" — Rachael suddenly looked at the note in concern. "You said this was all ready to mail?"

"Yes. I opened it to see what it was."

"Clara is the soul of ethics," Sadd murmured.

"Will the change still hold?" said Rachael. "I mean, now that she's dead."

"She wasn't dead when she made the change," I pointed out cleverly. "Why shouldn't it hold?"

"And if there's any hangup or holdup" — Sadd refilled our glasses — "you can always send the mission a check for the right amount, Rachael."

"True." She sat back again, relieved.

"And this is her bank book." I extended

it to Rachael. "And here is something I'm sure you've seen and will want."

I held up the picture of Grosse Pointe and Monte Carlo. Rachael reached for it lovingly. "You bet I want it." She glanced toward the stairs. "I'm running out of space, but I'll find a spot in my gallery right now. Come help me."

Sadd called after us, "Did Annette's flat yield anything else of interest?"

"Nothing," I said. I thought it best not to discuss Ungodly Plan till I had firmed it. It still wanted something. . . .

"Hold these." Rachael had removed two pictures from their hooks and was contemplating the wall. I looked at the two she'd handed me. One appeared to be a scene from some play, the other a shot of Herrick beside his car.

"I think . . ." Rachael held Annette's faded double frame against the bare spot. "Yes, it will go here in a nice new frame. I have about ten thousand of Herrick, so he can be sacrificed. So can Liam."

"Liam?"

"In the whiskers. It was some amateur play or other."

I thought of Herrick's words, "He's a frustrated actor."

Rachael was saying, "Wasn't Annette an

197

adorable baby? I was always scrawny."

Sadd was difficult the next day about what he called "the barbarous custom of the open casket." Rachael explained the reasons, but he was morose all the way to Ballsbridge, the area of Dublin where Brady's Funeral Home was located. Vee also seemed a little daunted. She confided to us that she'd never seen a dead person. Herrick said cheerfully that it was high time she was introduced to Irish wakes and that sometime he was going to write a humorous poem about them called "Doesn't She Look Lovely?"

Brady's was on a busy street but was blessed with good parking facilities. We pulled in at quarter past two — "visitation" was two to four — and ours was the only car. We were met by Mr. Brady himself with muted cordiality and were asked to sign the visitors' book. I looked at our five names and wondered when the sixth would be added. Would Boyd come? It was now almost two-thirty.

We were ushered into a long room lined with chairs. The open casket was at one end. We dispersed according to character. Sadd headed for the extreme end of the room, sat down, and took a book from his pocket. Herrick and Vee hovered near him for a few minutes, then disappeared. Rachael and I did what women of our generation have always done: walked up to the casket and stood gazing at a dear face.

Annette looked tinier than ever, engulfed in ruffled white satin. Her hair was fluffed, her little hands clasping a silver rosary were folded across the blue knit. On the bottom half of the casket lid was a bud vase with a single rose, which I knew to be Rachael's. She had specifically asked us not to order flowers, and the newspaper had so stated. Except for a few house ferns, the room was bare and dignified.

Rachael whispered, "I told them no makeup, but I think they've used a little."

"Not bad, though," I whispered back. I refrained from adding that Annette looked "lovely," wondering how many times we would hear Herrick's title phrase.

We backed away from the casket and sat down facing the door. Rachael said, "What time is it?"

"Going on three."

"He has an hour."

We sat in silence. I longed to take from my bag the pad and pencil I'd brought. Ungodly Plan was to take, in part, the form of a letter, and its composition required concentration. Impossible with Rachael sitting beside me vibrating with anticipation, wired to spring and escort Boyd to ringside.

Voices in the hall, and Mrs. Fermoyle and two middle-aged women came in, neighbors of "that nice Mrs. Pine, poor soul." We stood up to greet them, and Rachael walked to the casket with them. I eased away as the first "lovely" reached my ears, sat down, and started to scribble.

I wished for my husband, I wished for my son, I wished I knew more about the law. I got up and walked to the back of the room. Sadd said without looking up from his book, "It's after three. Want to bet?"

"No. What are you reading?"

"As if you cared. He won't show."

"He has to. If he doesn't it will look callous and unfeeling."

"That's a redundancy."

"Oh, shut up."

I wandered back down the room and sat beside Rachael again as Mrs. Fermoyle and friends rose from the kneeling bench and took seats across from us.

I said, "Sadd says he isn't coming."

"He'd just better."

Mrs. Fermoyle was gazing across at me, her round, pleasant face woebegone. Then I jumped, actually jumped as it hit me — the ultimately ungodly part of Ungodly Plan — and rushing upon it the knowledge that it could be blown if Boyd walked in. I took five steps across the room and whispered, "Mrs. Fermoyle, may I talk to you in the next room?"

A male voice in the hall made my heart sink. Mrs. Fermoyle said, "Oh, sure, Mrs. Gamadge — but there's Father. He'll be wanting to start the rosary."

Herrick appeared with a very young priest who looked around briskly and nodded to everyone. Now there would be introductions, a delay, and possibly Boyd's arrival. It was going to look awkward, even rude, but it had to be done. I seized Mrs. Fermoyle's hand with a "Please!" and almost hauled the poor woman to the back door of the room, through it, and into the hall. There was another room directly opposite, and it was empty.

"I'm sorry," I said, "I know this sounds strange, but would you mind missing the rosary for Mrs. Pine's sake? I have some really bad news. Please come in here and sit down."

Mrs. Fermoyle lowered herself onto a chair, her eyes on my face. The chant of voices in the ancient and comforting ritual of the rosary began in the next room. I closed the door, and it came to us muted but steady. I pulled a chair alongside the bewildered woman and said, "Mrs. Shea has learned that Annette Pine did not die from an accidental fall down her stairs. She was murdered."

Mrs. Fermoyle simply stared at me, and the dim chant reached us: *"Pray for us sinners now and at the hour of our death. . . ."* I hurried on, "The man we think did it visited her late that night. He doesn't know that he's suspected, and he'll probably be here shortly to pay his respects. He was a friend of hers."

"Friend?" The word was a gasp, followed by a whisper. "Why?"

"I wish I could give you all the details now, but there isn't time." I took her hand. "You can help us, Mrs. Fermoyle. You can help us prove that he did it. Will you? Will you, please?"

"Blessed art thou among women and blessed is the fruit of thy womb. . . ." She formed the words with her lips as they came to us, then said, "What can I do?"

I leaned over and kissed her cheek. "He mustn't see you here today, and it will mean not going to the funeral tomorrow."

"I can't anyways. I work mornings. I've had a Mass said."

"Fine. I'll call you tonight and tell you exactly what I want you to do. It will be tomorrow afternoon, and it's going to sound, well, maybe a little scary, but you'll be protected." I hurried on, "Of course say nothing about this to anyone. You live alone, don't you?"

"Yes."

"Is Mrs. Pine's flat rented?"

"Not yet."

"How did you get here today?"

"Mrs. Larkin drove us."

"She's one of the ladies in there?"

"Yes."

I stood up. "I'll tell her that Mrs. Shea has asked you to stay because she wants to talk to you. Now I'm going to call a cab. Please stay here till it comes, then we'll see you out the back door. And I'll call you tonight."

Mrs. Fermoyle looked up at me, pitiful but game. I put my arms around her. "I think you're wonderful. We couldn't manage this without you."

She murmured, clinging to me, "The poor, dear soul . . . such a nice lady, such a terrible thing."

I said, "I think I smell coffee. I'll bring you a cup. Promise you won't budge from here."

I went out and followed the aromatic smell to a steaming urn in an alcove. Prayers were over, and Herrick and Vee were standing there with the young priest.

"This is Mrs. Gamadge, a dear friend," Herrick said. "Father Gargan."

We shook hands, and I said, "What time

is the Mass tomorrow?"

"Ten o'clock. And my sympathy to you, ma'am."

"Thank you, Father."

I took the cup of coffee Vee had poured for me and went back with it to Mrs. Fermoyle. Then I closed the door on my treasure and peered into the waiting room. No sign of Boyd. Herrick and Vee descended on me.

"Clara, you've got something going!"

"What's up? What's up?"

"Later," I said. "Herrick, go in the office and call a cab. Tell them to drive it around to the back of this place — that's important. Vee, go out front and watch for it. Be sure it *does* go to the back. Then both of you get Mrs. Fermoyle into it. She's in that room. Be sure she isn't seen from the hall."

They radiated curiosity but took off. I walked back into the waiting room past Sadd, who murmured, "Three forty-five," and headed for Mrs. Fermoyle's neighbors. An elderly couple in tweeds were talking to Rachael, who beckoned to me to be introduced. Kind friends from Herbert Park. I excused myself as soon as was decently possible and turned to the two women.

"Mrs. Larkin?"

"Yes?" said one.

"We're going to ask Mrs. Fermoyle to stay here for a bit. Mrs. Shea wants to talk to her."

"Why, certainly. We'll wait."

Oh, Lord. "Well, actually . . . she's busy right now with some work Mrs. Shea brought regarding Mrs. Pine. I guess it couldn't wait. . . ." A few more phrases of glib nonsense, and I ended with, "Mrs. Shea's grandson will drive her home."

The ladies rose, and I went with them to the front door. It had a glass panel, and I saw a cab turn onto the drive. Boyd? We opened the door, and Vee hurried past me as the cab vanished to the rear. All I needed was to have them witness their friend's sub rosa departure. I kept them chatting on the narrow front porch with their backs to the drive till the cab reappeared and was gone. Then I released them.

I leaned rather weakly against the porch railing, looking out at the dense traffic with the feeling that I had plunged into it and was crossing against the lights.

The door opened and Herrick and Vee came out, she bearing a steaming cup, which she held out to me.

"You gave yours to Mrs. Fermoyle."

"Oh, thank you, thank you!" I gulped it greedily. "What time is it?"

"Four," said Herrick. "Our time's up.

Where is our other mourner? I use the term loosely."

I shrugged. Vee perched on the railing and said, "Aren't you going to praise us for not asking any questions when you know we're dying of curiosity?"

I touched her hair. "Praise you and thank you, too. Just let me get it all straight in my own head first."

"Sure, sure. Forget I mentioned it." She linked her arm in mine.

I looked up at the sky and said, "Is it always this nice in Ireland in September?"

"No," said Herrick, "it's staying pleasant in your honor."

I groaned. "I wish circumstances were pleasant, too."

"Christ, so do I." He thrust his hands deep in his pockets. "Mrs. Gamadge, promise me something: If nothing works out, you'll take Pix back to New York with you."

"I promise." I looked out at the street again. Those metaphoric lights were still against me, but I was halfway across. I said, "Herrick, has Boyd ever seen your friend Liam?"

"Liam?" He looked astonished. "I don't think so. Why?" Then quickly. "Dumb question — forget I asked. Let me think. . . . No, he has not."

"You're certain?"

"Certain. I've brought Liam out to Herbert Park once or twice, but never while Boyd was there."

I said, "Now for your 'why.' I'm thinking of staging a little drama with Liam in a leading role."

"My God, he'll love it. What about me? I'll take anything, even a walk-on."

"Me too!" Vee jumped off the railing.

"I'd rather use you both backstage. Will you ask Liam to call me tonight?"

"You bet I will!"

The door opened and Rachael's friends from Herbert Park came out. We said good-bye and went back inside. Our group gathered in the hall, where Mr. Brady was closing the visitors' book, looking rather mortified at the paucity of names. He handed it to Rachael and was instructing her on the next morning's procedure when the front door opened again.

A man stood there with the most enormous spray of flowers I had ever seen. He struggled in with it and handed the card to Mr. Brady, who gave it to Rachael. She frowned.

"I specifically said no —"

"I know you did, ma'am." He smiled a rueful apology. "But some people are so caring they simply *must*."

He walked into the room and set the atrocious thing on a stand before the casket.

Rachael had handed me the card, and I passed it to Sadd, who read it aloud.

" 'A touch of flu, but with you in spirit. Armand.' "

As we started to file out I glanced once more at the frightful tribute plunked under the little waxen nose of the Loved One.

18

None of us quite found our tongue till we neared home.

"I'll not have it on the grave," said Rachael as we turned into Herbert Park. "Can it be left in the cathedral?"

"Of course," Herrick said. "I'll ask Father Gargan to have it put on another altar after Mass."

The weather had apparently decided we'd been honored enough, for a cold rain had started. Sadd said, as we walked into the house, that a fire would feel good, and Rachael asked him to start one. I expected Herrick and Vee to go off somewhere, but they sat down with us and Herrick poured wine. Presently Vee said she'd like to make supper. Rachael thanked her — there was fish in the fridge. Herrick offered to help, and they departed. I was relieved. I didn't want to hit them quite yet with Ungodly Plan.

Rachael had sunk onto the big chair, her

face a mask of misery. I went and stood beside her, took her hand, and said, "Courage."

She moved slightly and squeezed my hand. I added, "I'm going to try something rather desperate."

Rachael sat up quickly. "It can't be too desperate for me!"

Sadd turned, blowing out the long fireplace taper. "I hope it doesn't involve chasing Boyd through the streets of Dublin in the Mercedes."

I stared at him. "No. Why on earth should it?"

"I have a confession to make." Sadd stood back and admired his blaze. "Martinis?"

We both nodded, and he went to the liquor cabinet. "I've been longing to drive that beautiful thing ever since we got here, but from what I've watched of the left-is-right-right-is-wrong syndrome, I have to admit I'd hesitate to take it around the block. Ice. Be right back."

"Boyd said the same thing," I remarked grimly. "I'd like to put him in it on New Year's Eve at midnight in Times Square. No, on second thought, he'd probably manage to kill ten people, total the car, and come out unscathed."

"What's the desperate plan?" Rachael asked eagerly as Sadd returned.

I said, "First — brace yourself — it involves calling Boyd and inviting him to come and stay here."

"*Clara!*"

"Listen to me, Rachael." I put both hands on her cheeks and turned her horrified face toward me. "He won't be here for more than a few hours if everything works out. But he must be invited, and he must move in tomorrow morning."

Sadd said, handing us drinks, "Now she's going to say 'Trust me.' "

"Damn right."

I kept my eyes on Rachael's face. She took a sip of her martini and said, "All right. But *you* have to call him. I really think I'd vomit into the phone."

"Glad to oblige," I said. "And the rest of the plan also involves phone calls. One to Mrs. Fermoyle —"

"Mrs. Fermoyle!" Rachael's horror was returning. "Clara, is it fair to drag in that poor —"

"She's already agreed and is booked into the show," I said calmly. "And a call to Henry. What time would it be in Brooklyn Heights?"

"Six here." Sadd looked at his watch. "Midday there. He'll be in his office to receive his mother's no doubt outrageous request."

"Worse than outrageous," I said. "Illegal."

Rachael suddenly caught fire. She sprang up. "Make the call at once, Clara! Use the phone in my room and tell Henry I'll pay all fines, court costs, and bail."

I beamed at her. "Give me the name and address of your bank."

She did so, adding, "Go, go, go to the phone! Go!"

I went, bearing my martini. I took my pocketbook from the hall table and mounted the stairs. Boyd's eyes followed me from a dozen places along the wall. I went into Rachael's bedroom, closed the door, and read the notes I'd made at the funeral parlor.

Three minutes later my son's voice said, "Mom! You sound as if you're next door."

"Next continent. Have you got ten minutes?"

"Hold on." He must have transferred to another phone, for in a minute he said, "More privacy. Fire away."

"Henry, Boyd has struck again."

"My God — who?"

"Annette."

"Who?"

Clara, you idiot! Henry had never heard of Rachael's companion, much less her connection with Boyd. Why hadn't I realized this and prepared a synopsis? Kicking myself, I floundered through the account. Henry asked a few questions and finally said, "Okay, I've got it. Mom, how can this man be stopped?"

"I think . . ." It was the first time I'd voiced my thoughts. "By destroying his morale. It's high now because he's sure he's fooled us all. I want to upset him, put him off balance without tipping my hand. He's in his seventies, he has a bum heart, and, as Sadd said, he's been onstage for several weeks without a break. I want to throw him a wrong cue that will make him blow his lines, then the whole scene."

"Nice metaphor. How?"

"Let me ask you a question first: Does your name or Tina's appear on your firm's letter-head?"

"Are you kidding? We're way down on the totem pole."

"I want you to write a letter to Rachael packed full of lies. Fax it, and send it to her bank tomorrow morning. It should arrive no later than nine."

"Am I to compose the lies?"

"No, I've done that." I laid the notes before me.

"And who signs this interesting document?"

"You do — with a fake name." I gulped my martini.

Henry coughed gently. "I don't want to sound picky, but you realize that if this letter ever —"

"It won't leave my hands for one minute, and it will be destroyed within an hour of its arrival."

"Okay. What do I say?"

I dictated slowly and carefully. Henry read it back, then said, "Do you want my honest opinion?"

"Of course."

"It's transparent as glass."

"I'm willing to bet not, given Boyd's mental and physical condition."

"There's that, yes. And the unexpectedness of it. What's the address of Rachael's bank?" I gave it to him. "And you want it tomorrow morning, nine your time?"

"Yes. We'll pick it up on our way to the funeral."

"Well, good luck. By the way, isn't there a famous prison in Dublin called the Mount Joy Prison?"

"I don't know."

"Check it out. You may be visiting me there."

We hung up, and I immediately dialed the Jury. Boyd answered his ring at once.

"Armand," I said solicitously, "how's your flu?"

"Thank you, Clara, I've been coddling myself, and I should be okay by tomorrow. I will *not* miss Annette's funeral."

"Your flowers were magnificent."

"The least — positively the least I could do."

I cleared my throat. "Armand, Sadd and I both feel, and Rachael agrees, that she must not be alone after we go. She'd like to take you up on your offer to move in here."

Keeping the elation out of his voice must have taken all of Boyd's acting skill. "Well, of course I'll be only too glad —"

"Why don't you pack up and come first thing in the morning? Then we can all go to the funeral together. Be here by nine."

"I'll pack right now."

I'll bet you will. "Oh, and Armand, there was a rather touching development today."

"Oh?"

"Having to do with Boyd."

"Oh?" A shade less casual.

"Annette's will. Rachael has it. That dear little thing left everything to Boyd. It isn't much — just a few hundred pounds in a savings account — but she stated that whatever she had was to be his with her gratitude for introducing her to her beloved friend, Rachael Shea. We just about cried, we were all so *touched*."

"Of course you were. So am I." His voice was quite level. "I wonder what happens when the beneficiary has predeceased the —"

"Oh, Annette took care of that herself. The money goes to some mission in Africa she supported. Very appropriate, of course, but a little sad when you think of poor Boyd just missing out on her generous gesture."

"Yes, it is sad. Well, see you in the morning. Good night, Clara."

Good night, Boydie. Sleep tight with that first little thorn of disappointment nestling in your side. He must be hurting badly for money at this point. Rachael's address book beside the phone gave me Mrs. Fermoyle's number. I rang it and we talked — that is, I talked for about ten minutes. She, good soul, finally said with a quaver that smote me, "Mrs. Gamadge, you do promise that there won't — that I won't —"

"Be in any danger? Not for one second."

You lie, Clara. For one, maybe two or three seconds. . . .

I went downstairs, deciding to hold out as yet on Mrs. Fermoyle's role but reporting Henry's. Sadd said, "I have to agree with Henry. It's transparent."

"No, it isn't," Rachael said, grimly. "Boyd's ripe for it." She started to pace the room, her tall frame and long strides rather a formidable sight. "Am I supposed to be expecting this letter?"

"Yes." I sat down on her chair. "You got

a phone call today from the law firm in Brooklyn, but you were too utterly depressed to take in what they were saying. You asked them to fax the information to you."

Rachael turned. "Who goes in for the letter?"

Sadd said, "Let's send Boyd. Poetic justice."

"Do I read it at once?"

"You give it to me. You're still too depressed to even look at it. I read it aloud, and we all start clucking about how sadly ironic it is, and we keep it up all the way to Brady's, by which time —"

"Boyd is going mad." Rachael held out her glass. "Sadd, I'll have another of those martinis."

"Me too," I said.

He filled our glasses, and we held them up in a salute. Sadd looked at us balefully. "You two remind me of the knitting woman at the guillotine."

"Knit one, purl one!" Rachael downed her drink.

But something she'd said gave me pause. I said, "I don't want Boyd to go *too* mad before I sic Liam on him."

"Liam!"

They both stared at me, and said Sadd, "How many persons have you rung into this production?"

Herrick appeared in the door, grinning. "Liam on the phone for Mrs. Gamadge. He wants to know if he has the right number for Central Casting."

19

The next morning fog shrouded Herbert Park and, according to the television, most of Dublin.

Sadd and Vee and I were drinking coffee in the kitchen when Rachael came down carrying a tweed coat and a man's gray sweater.

"One of Steven's, Sadd. For under your jacket."

"Thank *you*."

"Clara, you're to wear this."

I protested that my raincoat was ample, but she insisted agitatedly that it was not. I didn't argue. The poor woman bore all the marks of a sleepless night. My own hadn't been great, and Sadd had confided that his was right out of Edgar Allan Poe.

Vee apologized for having no dress to wear. Rachael said not to worry, the main thing was would she be warm enough.

"Oh, yes. This sweatshirt is heavy." It was navy blue and at least bore no quixotic legend.

"First thing you know, young people will be getting *married* in jeans," said Sadd.

"I have a friend who was," Vee said, and we laughed, which helped. Last night's late briefing session had not been conducive to jollity, and we all dreaded the arrival of Boyd.

Rachael put muffins on the table and said, "Herrick will be here in a few minutes with Rose. She cleans for me once a week. Annette always picked her up. Oh, dear, I'm sure she hasn't heard. Herrick will have to break it to her."

The Toyota rolled past the window, and a minute later a short woman wearing a heavy sweater and kerchief stood in the door.

"Oh, Mrs. Shea — I didn't know!"

"What a shock for you, Rose." Rachael went to her. "These are some friends of mine. Rose Mullins."

Rose nodded to us dolefully, then went for consolation to the broom closet. Herrick came in looking very spruce in a yellow shirt, striped tie, and corduroy jacket.

Vee said, "Wow. You look smashing."

"Too smashing for a funeral? Should I be more sedately clad?"

"On the contrary," said Sadd. "Bernard Shaw said we should wear our most glorious apparel to a funeral. After all, a soul has been liberated forever."

220

"I feel so scuzzy," moaned Vee. "I think I should stay home."

"You'll do nothing of the kind." Herrick pulled her to his side. "Stand in my smashing shadow and no one will notice you. Pix, when is you-know-who due here?"

"Any minute. We should be at Brady's by nine-thirty. Sadd, will you go out front and watch for his cab? We'll use it. From Brady's, of course, we four will be in the limousine. Herrick, you and Vee may as well go along."

Rachael had been moving restlessly about the kitchen as she marshaled her troops. Now she was still, leaning against the kitchen table. Sadd departed one way and Herrick and Vee the other. I went to my friend and put my arm around her, and we stood looking at the muffins. Rose asked if she could fix us some bacon and eggs — "trouble or no trouble, you must keep up your strength" — and we thanked her but declined the offer.

Sadd's voice called, "Cab waiting. Does Armand have time to take his gear upstairs, Rachael?"

She winced and I answered for her. "Yes, but hustle. Back bedroom. We'll wait for you in the cab."

Bags bumped aloft. I took Rachael's hand, and we went out and sat in the cab. A chilling fog enveloped everything, and I was grateful for Rachael's coat. I thought of our appalling ride to the hospital two days go, Boyd garrulous and cocky. I hoped he'd have the good taste to be silent. Well, cause for silence — black silence — was close at hand.

The men emerged from the house. Boyd was wearing a belted raincoat and a beret. Rachael murmured, "Pepe le Moko. I believe he's slipping. Armand never wore a beret in his life. When do I start my spiel?"

"Right now."

Sadd got in with us, and Boyd, blowing a quick, cozy little kiss to Rachael, climbed in front. He said officiously, "Brady's Funeral Home on Island Street."

"I know, sir."

"But we have a stop first," said Rachael as the cab pulled away. "At my bank. There's a letter waiting for me from some law firm in New York. Something to do with Annette. I don't in the least feel like looking at it, but I suppose I must. The Bank of Dublin, please, driver. Parnell Street branch."

Boyd said nothing, and no one spoke till we turned onto the parking lot of the bank. Rachael said, "Armand, will you be a dear and get it? Ask for Mr. Farrell. It's a faxed letter to me."

He got out and walked to the side door of the bank. My heart was beating uncomfortably, and Sadd hummed, a sure sign that he was tense. Rachael's freezing hand held mine. Now Boyd was back, a long white envelope in his hand. He gave it over the backseat to Rachael.

"Thank you, Armand," she said. "Now the funeral home, please, driver."

The thing lay in her lap. She said, her voice flat, "Read it to us, will you, Clara?"

I broke the seal, unfolded the crisp paper, and read aloud:

Mrs. Steven Shea
3 Herbert Park
Dublin, Ireland

Dear Mrs. Shea:

As I mentioned to you on the telephone yesterday, our branch office in Marseilles, France, is in receipt of information regarding a Mrs. Annette Pine. We were able to trace this person to an address in Portland, Maine. From there we received a letter from a Mrs. Thomas Jenkins, former landlady of Mrs. Pine, giving us your address.

We hope you are still in communication with Mrs. Pine and can help us. A relative of her mother's, recently deceased, has left Annette Pine a considerable amount of money as well as extensive real estate holdings in the Marseilles area.

Do you know of Mrs. Pine's whereabouts? If she is deceased, can you tell us if she left an estate of her own and who the beneficiaries are? The entire estate in France will go to them if they are living. If not, it will pass to The Children's Hospital in Marseilles.

I'm sorry to have intruded on what you explained was a "difficult moment" yesterday. We would very much appreciate your help in this matter.

Very truly yours,
Edwin Forrest

Even before I reached the end I started some gaspings and "Oh, no!"-ings. By the time I was finished Sadd had sat forward, his head in his hands, groaning such things as "Tragically ironic!" and "Poor old Boyd!" Rachael contributed, "Couldn't you just *weep?*" and "This is the saddest thing I've ever heard."

Boyd had sat motionless through the whole thing. The back of his neck was the color of clay.

I said, "Armand, did we ever think, as we sat waiting for him in the Dorrence, that this was just down the road for Boyd?"

"No. No, we certainly didn't."

His voice was very strange, and his effort to make it sound normal must have been tremendous. Something told me not to make him speak again. I folded the letter, put it in my pocketbook, and said, "You'll have to write them the sad news, Rachael dear. If it has to be this way, I guess the hospital in Marseilles is as deserving as the mission in Africa. But if only Boyd could have known that his kindness to Annette would bear such fruit!"

Sadd sighed. "Life is full of unexpected twists and turns."

"Boydie may have been difficult at times," said Rachael, "but we all loved him. I feel quite devastated."

And on and on till we reached Brady's.

The hearse was waiting for us, and just beyond it the Toyota. We transferred from the cab to the limousine, and Boyd went into the seat beside the driver like a man in a trance. Herrick came to our window and asked if all was okay. He greeted Boyd, who made a sound of sorts. The procession started.

More of foggy Dublin moved past us, and finally we were on Marlborough Street before the venerable Pro Cathedral. Our little group followed the casket with its little burden down the big aisle to a chapel of more merciful proportions. I made it a point to walk beside Boyd, who moved stiffly, looking straight ahead. His giant spray of flowers graced the altar step.

"Those are your flowers," I whispered. "Aren't they beautiful?" But I doubt if he heard me.

The Mass was very short, and again we followed the casket down the great aisle. Herrick came and walked on the other side of Boyd. Vee clung to my arm, and Sadd supported Rachael. As we emerged onto the wet pavement, I looked anxiously around at the flow of people who passed, stood, entered, or exited the cathedral.

Where was Liam?

Had I miscalculated the length of the service? Would he miss us? We couldn't stall indefinitely. The casket was already placed and the engine of the hearse started up. Our driver had opened our door. Herrick and Vee stood uncertainly beside his car, scanning the scene. Rachael and Sadd looked at me desperately. Only Boyd stood gazing into space.

Then Herrick, with a relieved look, nodded to me and called, "We'll go along." He and Vee got into his car as Liam came barging up, his face streaming perspiration, rumpled trousers flapping about his legs.

"Mrs. Shea?" he said, looking at me.

"I'm Mrs. Shea," said Rachael.

"One moment, ma'am." Liam lumbered over to the driver of the hearse, said something, the driver turned off his engine, and Liam lumbered back.

"Dublin police, Mrs. Shea." He waved an ambiguous-looking piece of plastic. "I'm Brendon Ahearne, plainclothes. We didn't want to alarm or embarrass you. Sorry to intrude at such a moment, but this can't wait. It has to do with the deceased woman, Annette Pine."

The word *police* had done something to Boyd's shoulders; one hunched and the other twitched. He turned and looked at Liam. I spoke up bossily.

"Surely it can wait! This is not a very —"

"It's all right, Clara." Rachael was calm. "Officer, these are my friends, Mrs. Gamadge and Mr. Saddlier, and this is my brother, Armand Evers. What's wrong?"

"It appears there may have been foul play in the death of this woman."

"Foul play!" I delivered a gasp.

"The person she rented a flat from — a Mrs. Fermoyle — saw a late night visitor there on the evening of the death. Fermoyle has been withholding this information through sheer fright but realized she had to come forward and tell us what she knew. She's extremely nervous about giving evidence and wants you to be present when she does. She says you know her."

"Of course I know Mrs. Fermoyle." Rachael had steadied herself against Boyd. "But — but I can hardly take this in. Could she be mistaken?"

"We have to look into it, ma'am."

Sadd contributed, "What was her information, Officer?"

"She believes she can identify the visitor — saw him come and go."

"Mr. Ahearne . . ." Rachael squared her shoulders bravely. "Tell Mrs. Fermoyle that I promise to go with you when you take her evidence." She moved, still holding Boyd's arm. "Now we must really —"

"Er . . . Mrs. Shea —" Liam shuffled after her. "We plan to see her this afternoon, but she lives alone and is quite terrified. She begged to be taken to your home for the questioning. Would that be an imposition?"

"I suppose not." Rachael looked around at us wanly. "We'll all be there won't we? Yes, come at four o'clock."

"Thank you, ma'am. Herbert Park, isn't it? Four o'clock."

Liam backed away, every inch of him protesting against leaving the stage, and Sadd helped Rachael into the limousine. I said, sotto-voce, to Boyd, "Armand, this is ghastly. Thank God we'll all be on hand. You didn't come a minute too soon." I gave him a little pat of commendation, and he walked around the car and got in front.

Sadd said, as we pulled away, "I vote we don't discuss this awful business right now. Agreed?"

"Agreed." Rachael put her head back against the seat with what I knew was genuine exhaustion. It engulfed me, too.

We rode in silence, our man of wood on the front seat leaning heavily to one side. The driver made an occasional comment; we were on our way to Glassnevin, a pretty area, he was sure we'd agree, if the fog lifted and we could see it. But it did not, and when we finally turned through a pair of iron gates, the words *St. Martin's Cemetery* were barely discernible over them.

We wound along a twisting, rutted road that appeared to drop sharply off on either side, for the tops of trees loomed. The hearse slowed to a crawl, as did we. There was Herrick's car. We stopped.

Father Gargan and the bearers got out. Our own driver was pressed into this service, and they bore the casket down the slope. We followed through the drenched and slippery grass, huddled together for support. I suddenly realized Boyd was not with us.

I panicked. Had he made a melodramatic exit through the fog, actor to the end? I eased away and scrambled a few feet back up the hill. Dimly I could see him through the misty swirl, still sitting in the car. I managed the rest of the climb and opened the car door.

"Aren't you coming, Armand?"

"I don't feel well." He looked straight ahead, rigid.

"Oh, I *am* sorry. Probably still a touch of that flu."

No need to worry that he might flee. I doubted he could move from the car without help. I turned and slid down the hill to join in the prayers.

20

Two hours later.

Boyd, recovered somewhat but moving like an automaton, had gone straight from the car to his room "to take a nap." Since his door closed we had taken turns watching the front and back stairs. Now I told Rachael and Sadd they could relax their vigil and put their feet up before the fire. I went into the kitchen, where Herrick and Vee were drinking tea. They jumped to their feet, and I put my finger to my lips.

"Now?" whispered Vee.

"Vee, dear," I said, "you can't come with us."

"Damn. But okay."

"Herrick has to drive me, and I want you here with Rachael."

"Mr. Saddlier's here," she said imploringly.

"Mr. Saddlier is not the person she'll need when I call to say it's over. He'll start quoting

231

Tacitus or somebody. What she'll need is a pair of arms around her. Besides, I have a job for you."

Besides, I don't want to further defile your memories of Ireland.

I went to the phone and rang Mrs. Fermoyle's house. Liam answered. I said, "How's her morale?"

"A bit shaky. And with such a great role! Now, if I had —"

"Liam."

"Sorry. When are you coming?"

"Now. Do we have a policeman — a real one this time?"

"We do. He's on his way. Officer Burns — a good friend of mine. I told him to bring a gun."

"I have to get off the phone. Boyd will need it to call a cab. They're leaving the kitchen clear for him. Vee will call us as soon as he leaves the house."

I hung up and Herrick said, "Let's go. We'll take the Merce."

Back through the murky Dublin streets we went. When would this be over? I'd come back to this city someday and enjoy even the fog; now it held only terror and questions. How long before Boyd would make some excuse to leave the house? What shape would his desperation take? Was he — ghastly thought —

following us even now?

As we pulled up before Mrs. Fermoyle's, Liam came out.

"Vee called. He's left the house."

"My God, how long ago?"

"Just a few minutes."

Herrick asked, "Did she tell you what he said to them?"

"That he felt better after his nap and needed exercise. He cut through the backyard to the next street."

"To rendezvous with the cab," I said.

A police car driven by a young officer pulled up beside us. Liam said, "Burnsy, park around the corner. The man we want is on his way."

The car pulled forward, and we hurried into the house. Mrs. Fermoyle flew to me. "Oh, Mrs. Gamadge, I'm that scared now. I'm not sure I can —"

"Of course you can." I hugged her with detestable cheeriness, feeling like a rat for subjecting her to this. "We'll be right in the next room, and here's a big, strong policeman" — the shortest, slimmest young man I'd ever seen stood in the door — "and it will all be over before you know it."

Liam greeted the officer and introduced him all around. Mrs. Fermoyle bewailed the sight of his gun and said she never thought she'd see one of them terrible things in her house and would anyone like a cup of tea.

I said, "There isn't time, dear, but go in the kitchen and make one for yourself. Stay there till you hear the doorbell."

Liam said, "I've been checking out good views of the parlor, and this little bedroom seems to have the best." He walked to a door. "Shall we adjourn?"

"Will this man be armed, ma'am?" asked Burnsy.

"Good Lord, no. That is — I can't imagine" — this gruesome possibility hadn't even occurred to me — "no, I'm sure he's never held anything but a prop gun in a play."

"He's an actor?"

"About to play his greatest scene," said Herrick. "Shouldn't one of us keep an eye peeled on the street?"

"I want to," I said. "I'll join you as soon as I see him."

The three men went into the bedroom. I heard Mrs. Fermoyle's kettle start to whistle as I took up a position behind the curtain of the front window. The fog had lifted somewhat, and there was decent visibility a block either way.

"I hope it won't be long," Mrs. Fermoyle called pathetically.

"It won't."

It was, in fact, about ten minutes. I had

mentally followed Boyd's progress on foot out of Herbert Park, his meeting with the cab, and its trip to the end of this street. It should be about now, I thought, and was rather proud of myself as a tall figure in a yellow slicker, hood pulled down over face, came striding down the wet pavement toward the house.

I left the window, and Liam admitted me, pushing the door almost to. Burnsy stationed himself at an inchwide view, Herrick, Liam, and I straining over his shoulder.

The doorbell was a cheerful chime, and Mrs. Fermoyle marched bravely from the kitchen and out of range.

"Mrs. Fermoyle?" Boyd's voice was hearty and pleasant.

"Yes?" Not a quiver, bless her.

"I'm a police investigator. It's about the death of your tenant, Annette Pine. I'm an American. They've asked me to come in on it because she was an American."

I hadn't known what gibberish he'd employ to gain entrance and told her to accept anything. Nice touch about being an American, Boydie. She might have questioned your accent.

"Please come in."

"I won't disturb you if anyone's here."

"No, sir, I'm alone."

They both came into view, the yellow

slicker steaming. I'd expected him to be quick, but not so lightning quick.

"Shall I make you a cup of tea?"

"Thank you."

She turned from him, and his terrible hands went out to her neck. She shrieked and collapsed. The men were upon him, and I rushed to the prone, hysterically sobbing Mrs. Fermoyle. Liam, with no business saying it, said, "Boyd Evers, we arrest you for the murder of Annette Pine and the attempted murder of this woman."

The "we" sounded absurd, and Burnsy looked at him with a near smile.

"I'm *Armand* Evers," Boyd said.

I dimly realized that he was looking not at them, but at me as I cradled Mrs. Fermoyle and helped her up and into the kitchen. I didn't want to see or hear anything more. I closed the door.

"You were *magnificent!*" I mopped the poor, blotchy face. "Sara Allgood never did better at the Abbey Theatre. Did I tell you that Mrs. Shea has a very special present for you? You can't imagine how grateful —"

There was a shout, a scuffle, a hideously loud report, and something smashed into glass. Mrs. Fermoyle cried, "Dear God, what now?" and I yanked open the door. The parlor window was shattered, and Boyd was backing out of the front door, waving Burnsy's gun. The three men stood motionless. Startled faces appeared at windows and doors across the street.

Boyd yelled, "Herrick! Throw me the keys to the Mercedes!"

Herrick yelled back, "Don't be an ass, Boyd! You can't drive that thing, and you know it!"

I tried to push past the men, but Burnsy held me back.

"Let him be, ma'am. That wild shot through the window did it — I'm almost glad he grabbed the thing. Somebody over there has already put in a call, you may be sure. He won't get far."

Liam said, "Better toss him the keys, Herrick."

"Give them to me!" I seized the keys from Herrick and, despite efforts to stop me, made a most unladylike charge through the door, landing on the walk ten feet from Boyd. A petrified crowd had gathered behind him.

I said, "Here are the keys, and you can have them if you want them, but do you remember when you and I talked about driving the Mercedes and you joked about taking your life in your hands? It isn't a joke now, Boyd."

"I'm Armand, Clara. Boyd's dead — remember?"

I looked into his mad eyes, and the words

I'd spoken to Henry flashed through my mind. "I wanted to throw him a wrong cue that will make him blow his lines, then maybe the scene." Well, the scene was blown with a vengeance, but his lines were pat to the end.

"The keys, Clara."

I held them out, and he snatched them. He backed toward the Mercedes, opened the door, and, still training the gun on us, got the keys into the ignition. The door was still open and one leg out when the car started. Now he pulled himself in and slammed the door. The Mercedes lurched forward into the path of an arriving police car and then, with that most sickening of sounds, into the car itself.

Oddly, both vehicles were salvageable. Boyd was destroyed by his own unsalvageable heart.

EPILOGUE

A year later almost to the day.

The same cottage, the same warm Cape Cod night enclosing the porch, the same shouts, plus two, coming from the water, Sadd in the same chaise, Rachael where Armand had sat, the infant in my arms this time Vee and Herrick's.

I put the bottle on the floor and lifted the baby to my shoulder. I said, "Sadd, don't be difficult."

"I thought we agreed not to discuss the wretched business."

"We did and we haven't," said Rachael, scooping ice cream. "It's just that we're leaving tomorrow, and if you don't mind my bringing up —"

"Rachael, dear, bring up anything you like. You too." I patted the baby's back.

"I didn't write you about a lot of things because, well, I was in a fog for so long, and then I couldn't remember what you knew or

239

didn't know. You had to leave so soon after, and all I could remember was that you'd saved my life and my sanity —"

"This is exactly what I mean!" Sadd sat up on the chaise. "I knew that if we got on the subject, you'd start this blather — my favorite Irish word, by the way."

"What does it mean?" I asked.

"Nonsense."

"Then Sadd's right, Rachael. No blather."

"Okay, no blather." She laughed. "Just this" — she took an envelope from the pocket of her robe — "and then I'm going down to that wonderful water with the kids. I was going to mail it, but then you set up this lovely visit and I decided to bring it." She extracted two slips of newspaper. "First, both obituaries."

We sat very still. Laughter drifted over the dark sand. Rachael went on quietly, "Armand's says simply — Herrick took care of this — that he died in a car crash in Dublin. Henry sent me Boyd's from New York. It reads 'victim of drowning in hotel pool.' Are we agreed not to unscramble?"

Sadd and I both said yes or something. Rachael took a bite of her ice cream and said, "I sent a copy of Armand's to his daughter. That girl is my niece, and I've never known her. For Vee's sake I'll try to stay in touch with her. She wrote me a lovely letter about her mother."

"Her mother?" Sadd looked puzzled.

I said, "If you would read your mail for its content and not to ferret out mistakes in syntax —"

"I remember." He snapped his fingers. "You wrote me about Rachael's magnanimous gesture."

"Pooh," said Rachael, "that poor woman is going fast."

"But going fast in the same expensive nursing home Armand kept her in — thanks to you." I rubbed the baby's heavenly cheek with mine.

"Now this" — Rachael took a little wad of clippings from the envelope — "I think will interest you most."

Something in her voice made me look at her quickly. Sadd sensed it, too, and sat forward.

"It was weeks — months — before I could make myself go through Boyd's things. His stuff lay up in that back bedroom, and I used to walk past it with a shiver. Finally one day I made a pitcher of martinis, drank a toast to you both, and went up and plowed through it all." She removed a paper clip from the yellowing wad. "I have to hand it to Boydie. The impersonation was remarkable. To all intents and purposes he was Armand Evers. Except for something Boyd Evers couldn't bear to part with. These."

Sadd stood up and took the clippings from her. He said, "His reviews. No actor will ever part with his reviews."

"They were in his wallet."

Sadd walked over to the one lamp on the porch and held them under it. He read a line here, a phrase there.

"West Dennis, 1946, 'Boyd Evers made the most of the thankless role of Amanda's husband. . . .' Cherry Street Theatre, 1950, 'ably supported by Boyd Evers as Dr. Regent. . . .' Papermill Playhouse, 1971, 'Boyd Evers stands out in a cameo performance —' "

"No more!" I wanted to cover my ears.

Sadd took the envelope from Rachael and dropped the treasured tributes into it. He said, "That brazier out there is still glowing with our cookout coals. Okay with you two?"

We nodded, and he went out and laid the envelope on the rack. It showed at first a half-hearted, pinkish hue, then flared red and consuming. Sadd came back in, dusting his hands, and helped himself to ice cream.

"Actually, 'cameo performance' is the wrong phrase," he said. "It should be 'cameo role.' Reviewers are so slipshod about —"

There was a gratifyingly loud burp from little Clara.

The employees of THORNDIKE PRESS hope you have enjoyed this Large Print book. All our Large Print titles are designed for easy reading, and all our books are made to last. Other Thorndike Large Print books are available at your library, through selected bookstores, or directly from us. For more information about current and upcoming titles, please call or mail your name and address to:

THORNDIKE PRESS
PO Box 159
Thorndike, Maine 04986
800/223-6121
207/948-2962